Blanton arrived, carrying his handcuffs in one hand, his revolver in the other. He passed the manacles to Longarm as he stopped beside the already-cuffed prisoner.

"I'll watch him while you take care of the other fellow," he said.

Longarm nodded. Holstering his Colt, he started for the second prisoner. The man began unbuckling his gun belt. He seemed to be having trouble with the big ornate buckle.

Longarm saw the outlaw slide the miniature revolver from behind the buckle. The man was bringing up the tiny weapon when Longarm drew and fired. As the heavy slug drove the outlaw backward, his fingers tightened and the little revolver spat.

Behind Longarm the other outlaw moaned. Longarm swiveled around to see Blanton turning, too. They watched the handcuffed bandit as he swayed, a trickle of blood seeping from the tiny hole just above his brow. He tottered for a moment, then crumpled to the ground.

Blanton's jaw dropped. He turned to Longarm and gasped, "Where the hell did that fellow you were cuffing find a gun so little?"

LONGARM

AND THE DEVIL'S STAGECOACH

JOVE BOOKS, NEW YORK

LONGARM AND THE DEVIL'S STAGECOACH

A Jove Book/published by arrangement with
the author

PRINTING HISTORY
Jove edition/March 1990

ISBN: 0-515-10270-9

Jove Books are published by The Berkley Publishing Group,
200 Madison Avenue, New York, New York 10016.
The name "Jove" and the "J" logo
are trademarks belonging to Jove Publications, Inc.

PRINTED IN THE UNITED STATES OF AMERICA

10 9 8 7 6 5 4 3 2 1

Chapter 1

In the heat of the muggy Kansas afternoon, the packed little courtroom was like a steam bath. Sunlight flooded in from the unshaded windows, and as the yellow beams of light crawled across the room and struck the men occupying the seats, they began inching toward the center aisle of the long narrow room to get out of the rays' sultry path.

Longarm was sitting in an end seat next to the center aisle, several rows distant from the judge's bench, and even though the sun's warm rays had not yet reached him, he could feel their heat. He turned to speak to the man in the seat next to him; though they were strangers, they'd quickly struck up a speaking acquaintanceship, exchanging names and occupations.

To Longarm's relief his temporary neighbor, Joe Glass, had proved to be a taciturn type who did not bedevil new acquaintances with unanswerable questions. After their initial name-swapping both men had been content to sit in silence. Even when Longarm had been called to the witness stand and had testified as to the details of Sam Carter's crimes and subsequent arrest, Glass had not asked questions.

Now Longarm turned to Glass and said, "It'd be a welcome relief if that jury'd come in before the sun gets on us."

"They sure have been out long enough," Glass agreed. He swiveled his head around as the courtroom door opened with a high-pitched squeak of hinges, then he nudged Longarm and said, "If you're interested enough to look around, that's Sam Carter's woman coming in right now."

Longarm was interested enough. During the long trip returning from Dakota Territory, where he'd trailed Carter and arrested him for the murder of a United States postal clerk during a train robbery, Carter's conversation had been almost exclusively about his love light, Nita Sneed. Moving as casually as possible Longarm swiveled his head to look at her, and now he could see for himself why Carter had talked as much as he had.

Longarm saw at once that Nita Sneed was past the prime of youth but was still young and attractive enough to draw men's eyes to her. She was tall without being obtrusively so. Her facial features were regular, composed of a thin nose with flaring nostrils, high cheekbones, full lips and a firm chin. The brilliant blue of her large eyes and the glow of her flawless skin, in addition to the bulge of slightly oversized breasts in a dress that was just a bit too clinging, would have drawn men's eyes anywhere she appeared.

2

"Nice-looking woman, ain't she?" Glass asked.

"Nice enough," Longarm agreed.

"Makes a man wonder why a damn outlaw like that Sam Carter couldn't go straight and settle down instead of killing and robbing and all like that," Glass went on.

"It does, for a fact," Longarm replied.

"What you figure the jury's going to do about that Carter fellow?"

"There ain't much else they can do but find him guilty," Longarm said. "You've been listening all along. How would you vote, if you were on it?"

"I'd say string him up." Glass nodded. "He didn't put up much of a case. What you figure's taking them idiots on the jury so long to make up their minds, Marshal Long?"

"Your guess is as good as mine," Longarm replied.

"Well, my guess is that they want to make sure they'll get paid for a full day today," Glass said. "But maybe it's just because sitting on a jury's got a way of making some folks feel like they're a lot more important than they really are."

"I'd say that's hitting the nail right on the head," Longarm said with a nod. "From what I've seen of people, something happens to 'em when they get on a jury. Seems like it makes 'em feel bigger than they really are."

"If it was left up to me—" Glass began, but stopped short when the door behind the judge's bench opened and the jury members filed out, followed by the court clerk.

"All rise!" the bailiff called. "This honorable court is now in session again, Judge Martin Leggett presiding!"

There was a moment of confusion as the men crowding the courtroom rose and fell silent. The judge emerged through a different door, followed by the sheriff and his handcuffed prisoner. A momentary wave of muffled voices rose from the men crammed into the small room as the sheriff led the manacled prisoner to the corner of the room behind the judge's bench. Then the judge stepped up to the side of his bench. Without sitting down he picked up his gavel and its sharp *ratta-tat* brought silence again.

"Gentlemen of the jury, have you reached a verdict?" the judge asked.

"We have, Your Honor," one of the men of the panel said.

"Very well." Leggett nodded and went on, "The bailiff will deliver the verdict to the court."

Now the silence of the courtroom was broken only by the thunking made by Bailiff Ed Henry's boot heels on the scuffed wooden floor as he went to take a folded slip of paper from the foreman and deliver it to the judge. Unfolding the paper, the judge scanned it quickly. His expression did not change as he turned to face the prisoner.

"We the jury find the prisoner guilty of murder without recommendation of mercy," he read. Lowering the paper Judge Leggett went on without pausing, "This verdict by the jury leaves me no choice. Therefore, Samuel Carter, I hereby sentence you to be hanged by the neck until you are dead, and order the sheriff to carry out this judgment within the next five days at the time and place of his discretion. May God have mercy on your soul."

For a moment the courtroom was totally silent, then

4

it seemed that everyone present began talking at once. Longarm turned back to Joe Glass.

"I'll bid you good-bye now, Joe," he said. "Seeing as how that fellow's going to get his neck stretched here in Hays, I won't have to take him back to Denver with me. Which suits me just as well. My chief in Denver's going to think I'm a stranger when I walk in the office door."

"Reckon you'll be glad to be going home, then," Joe replied. "Now, if you was to wait for the next stage that's going to the railhead, we might go down to the corner saloon and lift a glass together."

"That's real thoughtful of you," Longarm said. "But by the time I get back to the hotel and pick up my gear, I ain't going to have more than a minute or so to spare, and I'll need—"

He broke off when the sound of raised voices reached his ears from the aisle behind him. Turning to look for the cause of the commotion, he saw Nita Sneed trying to push her way up the aisle leading to the bench, where Sheriff Larten, still holding his prisoner with a hand on the condemned man's shoulder, had stopped to turn and exchange a word with Judge Leggett and the bailiff before leading Carter away.

"Looks like she's trying to get up to tell him good-bye," Glass said. "I reckon it'll be the last chance she'll get, at that. Sheriff Larten don't waste no time. He'll have that murdering scoundrel swinging at the end of a rope come sunrise."

Even while Glass was speaking, Nita Sneed broke her way through the thinning crowd in the aisle and moved to within a step or two of Larten and his prisoner. When the sheriff turned to bar her way, Carter saw his chance and took it.

In spite of the hampering manacles around his wrists, Carter yanked Larten's revolver from its holster. He triggered off a shot into the sheriff's back, and as the lawman pitched forward Carter swiveled and fired at Judge Leggett.

Longarm's Colt was out by then. The bark of its report sounded like an echo of Carter's. The outlaw had no chance for a third shot. He was turning to bring the weapon to bear on the bailiff when the slug from Longarm's revolver reached its target.

It was a quick shot but Longarm's aim was true. The heavy lead slug from the Colt whistled past Ed Henry and sped on to its doomed target. Carter was hurled around, his body buckling from the impact of the heavy bullet tearing through his ribs into his heart. Then he sagged slowly to the floor and lay still.

In the aisle, Bailiff Henry turned and bent over the fallen outlaw. A few of those who'd been sitting near the front of the room had reached one or another of the bodies and were kneeling beside them. There were tight clusters around both Henry and the bodies. Loud talk filled the air. There was such a confusion of voices, so many men trying to talk at once, that no single voice could be heard and understood.

Longarm had the advantage of being closer to the dead outlaw than most. He was one of the first to reach Ed Henry's side. He hunkered down and watched while the bailiff put a hand on the neck of the outlaw, feeling for a pulse.

"Now, there ain't no use in you doing that," Longarm said mildly. "He's as dead as anybody'd be that took a slug through his heart."

"All the same, I had to be sure," Henry replied. "And I guess you think I'm a damn fool, not even drawing when the shooting started, but I never made out to be no kind of gunfighter."

"You don't need to feel bad about it," Longarm assured him. "You ain't the first lawman that's got caught off guard, and it ain't likely you'll be the last."

"I guess the sheriff and judge are both dead?" Henry asked.

"As a doornail," Longarm replied. "Which sorta gives you the deck, Ed. But I reckon you know that."

"You mean Statute Seventeen?"

Longarm nodded. "I ran into it once a long time back, and there ain't any other state I know about that's got one like it. But Statute Seventeen says you're an officer of the court, which means you're the boss in this courtroom from right now until the governor appoints a new judge and sheriff. That'll take a while, if I know anything about it."

Henry's voice reflected both impatience and puzzlement as he asked, "What'm I supposed to do, then?"

"Why, that's up to you. But was I in your boots, the first thing I'd do is stand up and say the trial's finished and tell everybody in the courtroom to go on home. Then you and me can sit down and work out what all else there is to take care of."

"That makes sense," the bailiff agreed. Standing up, he raised his voice and announced, "All you folks that haven't got any business here, go on home or wherever else you feel like. As of right now, I'm closing this courtroom till I can get things sorted out!"

Most of the spectators, showing their reluctance by their facial expressions or their slow movements, began leaving. Within a few moments, only Longarm and Bailiff Ed Henry remained with the sprawled bodies of Sam Carter, Judge Leggett, and Sheriff Larten.

"I got to admit I feel better now that that bunch is gone," Henry told Longarm. "Now I can see where we stand a lot easier."

"It ain't really such a much of a job you got left to do," Longarm encouraged him.

"Maybe not," Henry agreed. "But up till now, all I've been doing is help chase crooks and keeping the court in order. All this other legal stuff is like it's Greek or one of them other foreign languages."

"Just look at it sorta one–two–three," Longarm suggested. "Sam Carter killed the sheriff and the judge, then I killed Sam Carter. I was just doing my sworn duty as a lawman, so that part of your case is closed. You can discharge the jury any time you feel like it, and have the county clerk fix up the vouchers to give them what's due 'em. And you can notify me that I ain't needed no more, so I can start back to Denver. That's what I'm mostly interested in right now. I figure to take the night stage to the railroad and—"

"Wait a minute, Longarm," Henry broke in. "I'd feel a lot easier in my mind if you'd stay here in Hays tonight, just in case I need to get you to give me a hand again."

"You don't need me hanging around," Longarm protested. "I don't see there's much I could do if I stayed. Anyhow, this is your territory. All I'd be doing is getting in your way."

"That's not the way I look at it," the bailiff replied.

"You know, when Pete Lanihan beat out Wild Bill Hickok for sheriff at that last election, nobody figured that Pete was going to up and die the way he did."

"Pete was a good lawman," Longarm said. "I worked a case or two with him."

"Well, after he died, and the judge put Tom Larten in as sheriff, I didn't have no idea that Judge Leggett'd talk me into taking on the bailiff job. Maybe you didn't notice it, the little time you've been here, but I don't know my butt from a hot rock about what to do yet."

"I ain't noticed you doing anything wrong," Longarm said. "But I don't guess it'd put me all that far behind to stay here in Hays another night. Tell you what, Ed. Let's finish up here and then go get a bite to eat. We'll visit while we're having supper, and if you got anything to ask me, we can hash it over. Then I aim to go to my room and get what shut-eye I can for what's left of the night."

When Longarm arrived at the Cattleman's Hotel—the name its overly proud proprietor had given to a slightly remodeled boardinghouse—the clock over the desk in the postage stamp–sized lobby told him that midnight was less than a half hour away. There was no one at the desk, but he'd long ago found it wise to carry the key to his hotel room in his pocket.

Mounting the short flight of stairs to the second floor, he opened the door and went into the small square room. As he entered, he scraped his iron-hard thumbnail across the head of a match and lifted it high to guide him to the nightstand. Lifting the lantern's glass chimney he touched the burning match to the wick and adjusted the flame until it stopped smoking.

Standing beside the table, Longarm reached for the bottle of Maryland rye that stood beside the lamp and took a healthy swallow. He stood for a moment trying to decide whether to follow it with a second swallow, then made up his mind to wait until he'd undressed and was ready to crawl into bed.

Unbuckling his gun belt, he draped it over the back of the nearest chair and moved the chair to the head of the bed. He placed it carefully, where the butt of his Colt would be within instant reach. He was studying the position of the weapon's butt in relation to the head of the bed when a woman's voice spoke from the still-open door.

"I don't suppose you'd object if I invited myself in for a little visit?"

When Longarm whirled to face the door, the butt of the Colt was nestled in his hand. For a moment he stared wordlessly at Nita Sneed where she stood framed in the open doorway, then he smiled and let his gun hand drop.

"I sure ain't one to find fault when a lady comes calling, even if she does catch me by surprise," he said. "Step right in and sit down. I'll move that stuff off the chair."

"Don't bother, Marshal Long," Nita told him. She was closing the door as she spoke. Turning, she walked past Longarm to the bed and sat on its edge.

"If we're going to visit, there ain't no reason to be formal," Longarm said. "I got a sorta nickname that I answer to, it's Longarm."

"I've heard it," Nita replied. "Sam mentioned you more times than I like to think about. But I don't hold grudges, Longarm. Sam played the fool today, and I haven't got any use for fools."

"I take it you don't put me in the fool class, or you wouldn't be here."

"Not likely. I woke up when I heard you coming up the stairs, and peeked out the door to see who it was," she went on. "Then I got to feeling sorry for myself. But I've felt that way before, and company always cures it."

"So you decided you'd pay me a visit." There was no inflection in Longarm's voice as he asked the question.

"I thought you might like some company, too."

"A lady's always welcome company," Longarm told her. "If you'd like a little sip of something, there's a bottle of prime Maryland rye on that table by the bed. Just tilt it up, if you got a mind to. It seems like this place don't furnish glasses."

"Later on, maybe," she said. "But right now. . ."

Nita let her voice trail off into silence as she began to free the line of buttons that ran from the neck of her dress to her shoulder. She raised her eyes to watch Longarm as she lifted her bared shoulder and shrugged while she tugged at the arm of the dress.

Freed from the confinement of the garment as she slipped it slowly down to gather in folds at her waist, Nita's full breasts with their dark rose-hued tips set in puckered pink rosettes drew Longarm's eyes like a magnet attracts steel.

"Now, that's as pretty a pair as I ever recall looking at," he told her. He was freeing the buttons of his shirt as he spoke. "And I bet I ain't the first one to tell you that."

"I won't lie and say no," Nita said. Her gaze was

11

fixed on his crotch. "And from what I'm looking at right now, I have an idea we're going to get along pretty well together."

Longarm reached her side while she was speaking and levered his feet out of his boots. Nita lifted her hands to caress his already-bulging crotch. Leaving one hand free to roam, the fingers of her other hand were moving nimbly, unbuckling his belt. She wasted no time in transferring her attention to the buttons of his fly, then yanked down the waistband of his trousers.

"Oh, my!" she exclaimed as she saw the bulge of Longarm's erection outlined beneath his long johns. "Now I'm sure I was right when I decided to pay you a visit!"

Longarm had finished unbuttoning the close-fitting balbriggans down to his waist. Ignoring the remaining buttons, he pushed them to the floor and stepped out of them. Nita stood up and shrugged to free herself from her dress. It slid from her waist to the floor with a soft rustle. She clasped her hands behind Longarm's neck and levered upward, spreading her thighs as she rose.

Quickly, Longarm positioned himself and thrust. Nita gasped as he drove into her. She clamped her thighs around his hips and pulled him deeper into her. For a moment they stood motionless, then Longarm shuffled across the few inches that separated them from the bed. He bent forward, letting Nita's weight pull him down to fall on top of her.

A gasp, almost a scream, escaped Nita's lips as Longarm's weight pressed her to the mattress. She locked her legs tighter and sought Longarm's lips with hers. For a moment they lay motionless, then Longarm began thrusting.

For a few minutes Longarm drove hard while Nita lay still, her thighs spread wide, fully accepting Longarm's lusty driving. Each time he ended one of his long deep penetrations a small smothered quivering sigh burst from Nita's throat and ended with a wordless gasp, then trailed off to a sigh that was part happiness, part moan as their bodies met with a fleshly *thwack*.

Suddenly Nita came to life. She dug her heels into Longarm's back and began rocking her hips with a twisting lift that brought them up to meet and match his steady strokes. Longarm could read the signs. He slowed the tempo of his stroking to a more deliberate pace until Nita's mounting frenzy ebbed. When her gyrations grew fainter and were no longer a series of convulsive heaves, he stopped moving and simply held himself in place, filling her.

"Don't stop!" she gasped. "I'm—"

Longarm pressed his lips to hers and slid his tongue in to meet hers. He was not thrusting now, simply holding Nita in place beneath him. The ripples that had been passing through her body slowly ebbed and stopped.

For a few moments neither of the pair moved, then Longarm started driving again. Nita was slower in responding this time, but when her quivering did begin her body shook with greater fury than before. Longarm was reaching his own peak now. He did not stop, but increased the force and tempo of his lusty thrusts.

When Nita started tossing wildly and was seized once more by a series of uncontrollable jerking spasms, Longarm speeded up, driving to his own climax. Nita began gasping as her hips writhed and tossed. Longarm was almost ready. He drove the last few moments until

Nita began crying out, a long wordless keening from deep in her throat.

For a moment she shuddered on the brink while Longarm raced to meet her. They were joined now in their final frenzies, gasping and quivering and tossing, and when Nita's keening cry began to subside Longarm drove quickly to his own climax. Suddenly Nita sagged as though she had no bones and Longarm's final gasps burst from his lips as he relaxed on her still-quivering body. Then both lay quiet and only the sound of their breathing broke the silent darkness of the room.

Chapter 2

"You're surely not getting dressed to go out at this time of night, are you?" Nita's voice from the bed was slurred with sleepiness.

"Not so's you'd notice," Longarm replied. "I just got up to light me a cigar."

As he spoke, Longarm fumbled a match out of the pocket of the vest he was holding in one hand. He rasped his thumbnail across its head, and the flare of light showed Nita sitting up in bed. The protruding tips of her generous breasts cast a dark arc of shadow on their rosettes, and her lips were still a bit swollen from Longarm's kisses.

When the match settled to a small dancing flame he puffed his cigar into a glowing coal, which provided the room's only light as he blew out the match. He watched Nita's face, a reddish blob in the glow from the tip of his cigar.

"I guess I'd better tell you something, Longarm," Nita said. "I didn't come in here just to get you in bed with me, though I've got to admit I enjoyed it. All I ever got from Sam Carter was a dirty look and a quick ride a couple of times a week.'"

"Why'd you stick with him, then? You sure acted interested enough when you came into that courtroom."

"I'm a money woman, Marshal Long," Nita replied. Her voice was serious now. "And Sam meant money. You know how outlaws toss their cash around."

"Sure. I've followed a lot of money trails to crooks that I've run down."

Nita went on, "What really brought me here was some kind of deal he'd cooked up with Sheriff Larten. When I visited with him in jail Sam told me all about it."

"Larten was doing business with Sam Carter?" Longarm frowned. "I always figured he was a real square shooter."

Nita shook her head. "Sam told me the whole story. The sheriff said he was too old to hold down his job. He was getting up in years and wanted to quit but didn't have enough money put by to carry him very long."

"And Sheriff Larten was ready to turn crooked to get it?"

"From what Sam said, he was."

Longarm had seen enough lawmen cross to the wrong side of the law to believe what Nita had said. He asked, "What else did he tell you, Nita? And I mean right from the start."

Frowning as she tried to recall, and talking slowly, Nita went on, "After the sheriff had Sam locked up for about a week he started dropping hints and, well, Sam could spot a mark as fast as the next crook. He had a way of worming things out of people, especially where a lot of money was concerned, and he told me this was a big-money job."

"I guess you know all the ins and outs of how this deal Carter cooked up with Larten was going to be worked?" Longarm asked.

Again Nita shook her head. "All I know is that it was a railroad holdup east of Hays, a train with a big gold shipment from the Denver mint. It has to be someplace close to Hays, though."

"How do you figure that?"

"After Sam explained things, it was easy to figure. He was sure that he'd get a hanging sentence when he went to trial. He said that with his record there wasn't any doubt about it."

"I got to admit he called the turn right," Longarm agreed. "And I guess he'd come up with some kind of scheme to keep the rope from around his neck?"

"He was always good at planning," Nita said.

"How did he aim to get away?"

"Sam told me that after the trial was over, the sheriff was going to sneak him out of jail as soon as the jailer'd left for the night. It'd be dark by then, of course. They intended to ride out along the railroad tracks to where two more of Sam's men were waiting, then pull off the holdup."

"And take off for the tall timber, or wherever they were going to hide out," Longarm added.

"There was a little more to it than that. Sheriff Larten didn't want there to be a trail leading back to him. He was going to bring Sam back here and lock him up again so the jailer would find him in his cell tomorrow morning."

"I can figure out the rest of it," Longarm told her. "The day before the hanging, the sheriff would let him make a getaway. But what happened to make the scheme go wrong?"

Nita shook her head. "I'd like to know that myself, but I don't guess anybody will ever know for sure, now that Sam's dead. Maybe he thought the sheriff was going to double-cross him. Maybe the men he was looking for didn't show up. But maybe they're out along the railroad tracks right now, waiting for Sam to join them. The train carrying the gold's not due to pass through for another three or four hours."

"Well, I guess I've got it all clear now." Longarm nodded. "You're sure that's all you know about it?"

"I'm sure," Nita replied. Then she went on, "And I've been answering your questions for quite a spell, Longarm, plenty long enough for you to've got your second wind. But if you feel like getting back in bed with me and giving me as good a ride as you did before, I just might recall something else."

In the darkness ahead a faint reddish gleam no bigger than a man's hand was Longarm's first clue that he was getting close. He'd been traveling slowly through the moonless night, riding parallel to the tracks, and he judged the fire to be far enough ahead to allow him to ride a bit closer before pulling up for a final stealthy advance on foot.

As he moved forward, circling away from the tracks now, Longarm reined his livery mount to a slow deliberate walk across the flat Kansas terrain. It wasn't part of his plan to let the train's headlight make him a silhouetted target for the outlaws he was sure had kindled the fire ahead.

Although the night was moonless, the stars were bright and the flat featureless Kansas prairie offered no cover except the ankle-tall shortgrass. This didn't worry Longarm; he knew that the night vision of the men sitting by the fire would be much less acute than his. Noise was another matter. The night was windless and the waiting outlaws would certainly hear hoof clops sounding through the darkness if he tried to pass too close to them.

Moving in a semicircle away from the tracks, Longarm rode slowly until he was well beyond the fire. Now it was the men lounging beside the small blaze who were silhouetted, and he could see for sure that there were only two of them. Neither of them gave any sign that they were aware of his passage. When he'd put enough distance between himself and the waiting outlaws, Longarm turned back toward the rails.

He'd covered almost two-thirds of the distance on his way back to the rails when a patch of blackness on the shortgrass prairie caught Longarm's eyes. He reined toward it and found that it was what he'd been hoping for: a small patch of scrub oak, rare on the grassy Kansas prairies. Pulling up his horse, Longarm dismounted and tethered it to one of the small scrubby trees—few of them were more than head high to a man on foot—that grew at the edge of the clump.

Wishing for his rifle, but not greatly bothered by being forced to do without it, Longarm started walking toward the still-visible glow of the outlaws' fire. Shielded by the moonless darkness, he was sure that he needed to take no precautions against being seen until he was near enough to the blaze for the men sitting beside it to glimpse his silhouette against the clear star-filled night sky.

Longarm moved steadily but slowly. In his own ears the swish of his boots as he walked across the grassy prairie sounded very loud indeed, but he knew that it was not the sort of noise that traveled well. When he could begin to hear the murmur of voices from the two men beside the little blaze, he slowed his pace. After moving a bit closer to the fire he stopped and stood listening for a moment. Now he could hear the babbling voices of the pair beside the fire, but he was still too far away to catch anything but an occasional word.

He continued his steady progress at an even slower pace. When he reached a point where he could hear them clearly he was still veiled by the darkness that shrouded the prairie beyond the gleam of the little fire.

". . . don't like it a damn bit," one of them was saying. "Sam oughta be here by now. It ain't all that far to Hays."

"Don't go getting the willies," his companion replied. "You know Sam. He always shows up for a job at the last minute, but he always gets there in time."

"I reckon so. But one thing's certain-sure. That train ain't going to wait for him to show up. This is the only chance we'll have at it."

During his long stealthy approach to the fire, Longarm had worked out his plan. The few words he'd just heard were enough to convince him that Nita's story was true.

Raising his voice to a shout he called, "You men by

the fire! We got you surrounded! Make one move and you're dead!"

For a fraction of a second Longarm could not be sure that his bluff was going to work. The men beside the fire started to draw, but their awkwardly sprawled positions hampered them, and before they could straighten up Longarm sent a shot from his Colt into the little blaze. The slug scattered the burning twigs and showered the outlaw pair with coals, and they leaped to their feet, their clothing dotted with burning sparks.

Longarm fired again. This time his slug thunked into the baked soil between the pair, and the men raised their hands. Almost before the loud flat boom of the Colt had died away, Longarm called out, "All right, boys! You keep 'em covered, and I'll get their guns!"

As Longarm approached the outlaws he saw them hopping around in an effort to shake off the live coals that had landed on them.

"Toss your guns on the ground before you start putting yourselves out!" Longarm commanded.

Still more concerned by the dots of flame that were now growing larger on their shirts and trousers, the pair obeyed. They lifted their revolvers from their holsters and dropped the weapons at their feet. Even before the pistols had hit the ground they were beating at the little circles of red that were scattered over their clothes.

Longarm took advantage of their preoccupation by moving up to the fire and kicking the two revolvers away where they would be out of reach of the outlaws. A few of the burning coals that had scattered from the small fire had started blazes in the dry prairie grass along the right-of-way and were threatening to start fires, but they offered no immediate threat.

21

Taking the risk that the fires would not spread quickly, Longarm holstered his Colt and slid his handcuffs from his belt. Grabbing the arm of the man nearest him, he snapped one of the cuffs over his right wrist. Dragging his prisoner with him, he took the one short step necessary to reach the second outlaw and grasped the man's right arm. Then he closed the other manacle over the second man's wrist.

Longarm's moves had been so well planned and so fast that he'd completed them within the span of little more than a minute. The outlaws had been busy extinguishing their burning clothing, and even after the manacles were in place they did not quite realize what had happened to them until they both tried to turn and face Longarm.

To their surprise and consternation, they found that they were unable to do so. Coupled as they were, right wrist to right wrist, they discovered quickly that if one faced Longarm, the other must stand facing away from him, or be forced to take an awkward posture with one arm stretched across his own chest.

For a moment Longarm watched them turning and jockeying as they tried to do the impossible, then he said, "There ain't a way in the world that what you're trying to do'll work out, so you two might just as well give it up."

"Who the hell gave you the right to jump us?" one of the men demanded.

"My name's Long. Deputy United States marshal," Longarm said. "And you're both under arrest."

"Now, damn it!" the man who'd spoken complained. "You got no call to jump on us! Damn it, you oughta be able to see that all we are is a couple of peaceful cowpokes out looking for a ranch that'll give us a job!"

"I'll tell you what I see," Longarm replied levelly. "I see a couple of hard cases waiting for their boss to get here and work out how they'll go about holding up a train that's hauling a baggage car loaded with gold from the Denver Mint."

"Ah, hell!" said the outlaw who until now had been silent. "I didn't tumble to you when you called your name just now. You got to be the one they call Long-arm."

"I've been known to answer to it," Longarm replied. "And I got two pieces of bad news for you. One is that Sam Carter's dead, so he won't be showing up. The other one is that just as soon as you two mosey around and stamp out them little grass fires before they spread too bad, we'll be heading for Hays and jail."

"And that's the way it finished up, Billy," Longarm said in winding up his report to Chief Marshal Billy Vail. "The fellow I told you about has got my statement and all, so I won't have to go back to Hays and testify when them two outlaws go to trial."

Vail nodded absently. He was digging into his desk drawers, lifting out sheaves of papers bound with the narrow red tape that marked them as having come by mail from Washington instead of being transmitted by the telegraph that was reserved for more urgent communications. Longarm was no stranger to his boss's office routine.

"Now, hold up a minute, Billy!" he protested. "Every time you pull out one of them stacks of papers from back East, I know what you're figuring! It's some kinda

23

special case that you aim to put me on next. Am I right?"

"Right enough to fit," Vail agreed.

"And when you give me one of them specials, it means I'm going to have to start right out again before I can catch my breath," Longarm went on. "Where'll I be heading?"

"Down south to Arizona Territory. Which means you're likely to be keeping warm in the sunshine about the time we get the first snowfall here."

"Arizona Territory covers a pretty good chunk of land, Billy. Where exactly will I be heading?"

"I'll get to that in just a minute," Vail promised.

"Now, look here, Billy," Longarm went on. "I've been away more than a month chasing that Carter fellow and closing the case you gave me on him. I'd sure like to stay here in Denver for a while. I need to get some laundry done, and it'd be right nice if I could sleep in my own bed for a change, and—"

"Why, you won't have to leave on this new case right this minute," Vail said. "Take a day or two, have your laundry done and tend to whatever other chores you need to do. Now if that's settled, let's get on to this new case."

"Wouldn't you rather wait till just before I leave, Billy? I can puzzle over the case on my way to wherever it is you're figuring to send me. All you've said so far is Arizona Territory."

"I'd like it better if you started thinking about it now," Vail said. "Mainly because of the letter that came with this file."

"I guess if it's that all-fired important, you might as

well trot out them papers. You got me sorta curious, now."

Vail stripped the red tape off the sheaf of papers and began leafing through them. He said, "I can give you the meat without any trouble, but you'll need the bones, too."

"Body, bones and blood," Longarm agreed. "Go on, Billy, I'm listening."

"Well, now," Vail began, "you haven't been on a case in Arizona Territory for a while—"

"Not since I got mixed up with them Papagos," Longarm broke in. "And that was right close to Arizona Territory's belly button. Where is this case?"

"A good ways southeast of Papago country," Vail said.

"Close to what? Name a town, so I can have a place to tie to," Longarm suggested.

"Tucson's the biggest town close by, but the place you'll be heading for is east of it, closer to the New Mexico line than Tucson is," Vail went on. "From what I gather there's not much to this town you're going to, except that it's got a silver mine and a smelter that handles first-run ore. After the ore's been slagged out they send it to the big smelter at Lordsborough for the final run that turns out the ninety-nine-percent pure silver."

"Lordsborough's in New Mexico Territory, as I recall." Longarm frowned. "It seems to me that hauling the rough-run ore all that long way is just wasting time and money."

"That's not for you or me to say," Vail reminded him. "If it suits whoever runs that mine, it's their business. The reason we're mixed up in this is to find out what happened to the government vouchers the mint sent

25

back to the mine after the last silver shipment was delivered about a month ago. Those vouchers were signed, and they're just as good as cash money to whoever gets them."

"If I take you right, Billy, what you're saying is that somebody stole them," Longarm said. "But it seems to me that they'd be able to track 'em."

"That's the odd part of it," Vail said. "The vouchers never have been cashed."

"Then whoever's got 'em is just sitting tight, waiting for the fuss and foofaraw to die away."

"That's what the Arizona Rangers think," Vail agreed. "And it's why they've asked us to step in. Not that we wouldn't've put a hand in anyhow, since Treasury payments are involved."

"And nobody's got any ideas about who stole the vouchers. That's what it boils down to?"

"There's more to it than that," Vail corrected. "The vouchers went from the mint here down to Lordsborough, and there was no trouble with that. But when they were sent on from there to the mining town in Arizona, they just plain disappeared—along with the stagecoach carrying them. Whoever it is that stole them was dead serious about getting what they wanted. Now you've got to get down there and get them."

"Which reminds me of something," Longarm said. "A minute ago, I asked the name of the town where that silver mine is. You never did mention it."

"Maybe I'm just a little bit superstitious," Vail replied. "The name of the town is Death."

Chapter 3

Longarm's jaw dropped and he stared unbelievingly at Vail for a moment. At last he asked, "I did hear you rightly, didn't I, Billy? All you said was 'Death.'"

"That's all I said," Vail grunted. "Death. That's the town's name."

"Now, I've passed through Death Valley a time or two," Longarm went on, "but that's way out in California. Do you mean to sit there and tell me there's a town by that name, too?"

"Unless the Treasury Department's made a mistake, there is," Vail replied. "But I looked on the map when I got the file from Washington. If there really is a town by that name in Arizona Territory, it's sure not on there."

"Then how in tunket do you expect me to find it?"

"About the best thing I can think of for you to do is get off at the Southern Pacific railhead at Lordsborough, which is down in the southwest corner of New Mexico Territory, and start asking questions."

"Which is what I'll have to do, anyhow. Damn it, Billy, I got brains enough to do that. And I know about where Lordsborough's at. But this other town—"

"Death," Vail repeated. "You'll find your way there soon enough, I expect. That stage and those vouchers have got to be somewhere out there."

"Anybody that can't find something as big as a stage-coach ain't fit to pin on a lawman's badge, Billy," Longarm retorted. He stood up as he went on, "I'll take a day or so and get my laundry done and get my guns checked over. As I recall, Arizona Territory ain't real settled up down where I'll be going."

"It's pretty well deserted, I'd say," Vail agreed. "I'll have the clerk fix up your travel papers and vouchers. You can get started any time you're ready."

After the cool air of mile-high Denver, and the equally mild chill of New Mexico Territory's high plateau country from which the train had just descended, the windless sunrise air at Lordsborough was uncomfortably hot for such an early hour. Longarm felt sweat popping out on his forehead the minute he stepped off the train. The conductor was standing on the station platform, watch in hand. A second man—Longarm guessed he was the station agent—stood beside him. Longarm picked up his rifle and saddlebags before stepping up to the pair.

Before he reached them the conductor waved his arm in the universal railroad signal for highball and the train's whistle sounded the two quick blasts that indicated it was pulling out. The conductor swung aboard as the string of cars began to move slowly ahead.

Now Longarm could see the little town of Lordsborough that had been hidden by the coaches. He stood for a moment, looking at it. Except for the huge brick building with a towering smokestack that stood a bit away from the town, it could have been any one of two dozen other young settlements that Longarm had visited in the ever-changing west. He turned to the man who'd been talking to the conductor.

"You'd be the station agent, I guess?" Longarm asked.

"Sure am." The agent glanced at the saddlebags dangling from Longarm's side and the rifle tucked into his elbow as he went on, "I hope you didn't just find out that you left your suitcase or something else important on that train. If you did, I'll have to wire ahead to the baggageman at Winslow or Flagstaff and have them send it back. It'll be up to you to pay for the message and the shipping charges."

"Don't get upset, now. What I got here in my hands is all the baggage I'm toting," Longarm said. "But I do need to find out from you what time the westbound stage pulls out."

"Why, it left yesterday. Won't be another one for a week or so."

"I thought there was one that met every train?"

"That was before one of the stages just up and disappeared. The old boy that runs the stagecoach line ain't got but two coaches, so anybody that's traveling from the railhead here has got to wait."

"But if he don't feel like waiting, I guess he could hire a horse and keep moving," Longarm suggested.

"Oh, sure."

"Well, if you can tell me where there's a livery stable

29

here that I can hire a horse from, that's just what I'll do. But I'm sorta curious about that big building yonder. Looks to me like it's a smelter."

"It is."

"From the smoke it's making, business must be pretty good."

"I ain't heard any complaining. They was figuring on putting it up in Silver City, but about the time they was ready to start, the lodes there begun petering out, so they built it here instead."

"Well, this ain't getting me to that livery stable," Longarm put in. "And I still got a pretty fair ways to go."

"I'd say your best bet's the big one that's right at the end of Main Street," the railroader said. As he spoke he raised his hand and pointed. "Just step across the tracks and go that way. Keep on right through town and you'll smell the livery after you've gone a little ways. Once you get a whiff of it, just follow your nose."

"Thanks." Longarm nodded and turned, crossed to the rutted street and began walking in the direction the railroader had indicated. It was still very early and the town was just awakening. Only a half dozen people were straggling along the street and most of the stores were still closed. There were no swinging doors on any of the places he passed, but after he'd gone a short way the aroma of hot grease caught his attention. Looking ahead, Longarm saw a sign, CAFE, above one of the buildings he was approaching.

When he reached it he went in and found that the restaurant was as deserted as the street. He ordered ham and eggs from the sleepy-eyed cook, waited while the man prepared them and ate quickly. Then he resumed his walk, and as the railroader at the depot had predicted, Longarm's nose told him that he was getting close to his objective.

He reached the stable, looked around, saw nobody and went inside, where he found a man forking hay into the feed troughs. He did not notice Longarm as he entered, but kept working at the end stall. There were only three horses in the stalls that stood along the walls, and while he was walking toward the attendant Longarm made a mental choice from the trio.

"I reckon I can pick out any one of them nags?" he asked when he reached the attendant.

"I reckon." The liveryman stuck his hayfork in the dirt floor and leaned against it as he spoke.

"Likely I'll be needing it a while," Longarm went on as he took out his sheaf of vouchers. "And I'll want saddle gear, too. A McClellan, if you got one handy."

"Sure. Saddles cost two bits a day extra, though."

"I'd say that's reasonable," Longarm said. He took a voucher from his supply and handed it to the attendant. "I guess you've seen some of these before. It's a government voucher, good as cash when you take it to the post office. Except it ain't worth a thing until I sign it and fill in how much you'll get. I'll do that when I get back to turn in your nag."

"I've seen a few like it before," the liveryman informed him. "And I guess you wouldn't have any if you wasn't a gov'ment man. You want me to saddle the nag for you?"

"If it's all the same to you, I'd as lief do it myself," Longarm replied. "Just bring me that saddle and I'll get busy."

While he waited for the saddle, Longarm led the

horse he'd chosen out of its stall and gave it a quick looking over. It seemed sound enough, and tractable. The attendant returned with the saddle gear and stepped aside while Longarm got busy. After he'd finished his quick job of getting the horse saddled, Longarm turned to the liveryman, who'd been standing watching him.

"There's a town called Death someplace around here," he said to the liveryman. "I reckon you can tell me how to pick up the trail to it?"

"There ain't all that many trails from here to any-place," the man replied. "And there ain't so many folks heading for Death that they crowd the road there, nei-ther. You being a gov'ment man, I reckon you might be looking for that stagecoach that dropped outa sight? I expect it had a mailbag on it?"

"Maybe there was and maybe there wasn't," Long-arm said. "In the job I got a man don't answer too many questions if he wants to go on working. My job's to ask questions."

For a moment the liveryman stood silent, his brow furrowing as he thought over Longarm's noncommittal response. Then he nodded and said, "I guess I take your meaning, friend. But that stagecoach dropping outa sight the way it did has been about all anybody could talk about."

"It is something that don't happen every day, I'll agree," Longarm said with a nod.

"Sure," the liveryman said. "Well, if you'll just step outside with me, we'll move outa the way of the build-ing and I'll do the best I can giving you some direc-tions."

Longarm followed him to the edge of the weather-beaten stable, where the liveryman pointed southwest to a ragged cluster of hills. "You see that one hill that stands up higher'n the rest? That's Pyramid Mountain. Keep it on your left and about the time you get even with it you'll come to a place where the trail swings toward the west. That'll take you up over Antelope Pass, and where the trail forks at the bottom of the pass you take the right-hand branch."

"About how far is it?"

"Oh, you'll be hitting the turnoff about sundown. If you don't mind riding a little ways at night, you'll get to Death in time to have a late supper, if the hash house ain't closed."

"Thank you kindly," Longarm said. "And like I told you, when I bring back the nag I'll sign that scrip note I gave you. Then you can just take it to the post office and get cash for it."

"Like I told you," the liveryman said, "I've seen 'em before. So I'll just look for you when I see you ride in."

With a good-bye flick of his hand, Longarm slapped the reins and toed the horse ahead. He let the rawboned animal set its own pace across the barren, sunbaked, adobe-colored earth. The only time he touched the reins was when he noticed the horse veering away from the faint trace that led to the highest of the mountaintops that formed the jagged line of the horizon.

Longarm was no stranger to arid terrain. There were few places between the Rockies and the Pacific Ocean where his job had not taken him, though a number of years had passed since he'd been on a case in Arizona Territory. Long ago he'd learned that patience rather than speed was the secret of successful travel in arid, sunbaked land such as he was now crossing. He relaxed in the saddle, his eyes skimming the rugged landscape, but always returned his attention to the faintly marked trail that zigzagged up the rise in front of him.

A bit sooner than he'd anticipated, Longarm reached the crest of the gentle upslope. Though the grade had not been especially hard, the livery horse was beginning to breathe heavily, and he reined in to give the animal a rest. The downslope stretched ahead of him. It was much rougher country than he'd expected to see. The land supported little vegetation, though here and there were dark patches of low-growing brush, and less often he saw stands of scrubby dry-growth pines scattered across the yellowy soil.

Between the blotchy green areas where the trees were thickest the winding rims of shallow gulches zigzagged across the ocher earth. Longarm could see the road stretching below him, winding between the green pine stands and the arroyos that broke its surface in dark barren blotches, following the changes in the terrain. His mount was no longer panting now and the downslope promised easier going. He toed the horse to a faster gait as it started down the long incline ahead.

Longarm had traveled about a third of the way down the gentle slant of the zigzagging trail when the unmistakable high-pitched singing of a bullet broke the quiet air inches above his head. Sounding like the brief buzz of an angry hornet, the thin screech had not yet died away before the sharp crack of muzzle blast echoed from somewhere down the slope.

Even before the shot's fading echoes died away Longarm began to scan the downslope. He saw a thin thread of yellowish gunsmoke as it rose into the clear air, and before it had dissipated he was grabbing his Winchester from its saddle scabbard and rolling off his horse. The unseen sniper loosed another shot before he'd landed.

Like the first shot, this one was high. Stretched flat in his new position, Longarm could no longer see the pines from which the shot had come. He rolled to the edge of the trail, his eyes searching the slant below. Belly-crawling, pushing his rifle ahead of him, he wormed his way down the slope a short distance until he was in the brush. The strip of waist-high prairie grass was barely wide enough to cover him as he wormed through it. Nothing stirred on the long downslope.

"Old son," Longarm muttered, "there's got to be somebody holed up down there. The rifle that'll pull its own trigger ain't been made yet. All you got to do is wait till whoever it is comes outa cover."

He did not have long to wait. Only a few moments ticked past before a rider emerged from a clump of thin first-growth pines that lined the edge of an arroyo perhaps a half mile down the slope. The horseman left the trees at a gallop and started zigzagging away from the road. Though Longarm's Winchester was in his hand and ready he did not shoulder it.

At best, downhill shooting was tricky, especially at the distance between him and the retreating rider, who was pushing his mount in a fast zigzag through the growth of scrub pine on the far side of the arroyo. Instead of taking a quick uncertain shot, he studied the retreating sniper. By this time the fleeing man had abandoned his zigzag tactic and was bending low over his horse's neck, thumping its sides with his boot heels.

"Now, there goes a real nervous man," Longarm told himself as he slid a cigar out of his vest pocket and touched a match to it. "There ain't no way he could've known who he was shooting at, that's for sure. Nobody's got eyes that good. But one thing's certain: he was up to something that he didn't want to get caught doing, or he never would've let off that round before he began running away."

Levering himself to his feet, Longarm went back to his horse and swung into the saddle. He reined the animal off the trail and toward the arroyo where the sniper had been concealed. As he drew closer to the deep wide gap in the generally unbroken terrain, he noticed a strangely alien path that was almost parallel to the course he was taking himself. He wheeled his horse to get closer to the wide swath of broken and disturbed ground.

"Them wide wheels had to be on a big wagon of some sort," he muttered thoughtfully as he studied the grooves. "Could've been a freight wagon, or it could've been a stagecoach. Whatever it was, it had a good-sized load. And the tracks stop at the arroyo, which is likely where it's hidden and why that fellow was down there. Question is now, who in tunket is he and what would he be doing down in that gully?"

By this time Longarm had gotten close enough to the arroyo to get occasional glimpses of some sort of hulking object that the edge of the gully still concealed. He broke through the ragged growth of stunted pines that grew away from the line of its edge and an involuntary gasp escaped his lips.

Now Longarm could see the details of the strange sight that met his eyes as he gazed into the little ravine. He was looking at a battered stagecoach lying on its side at the bottom of the gully. The door on the upturned side of the vehicle had been opened and was resting on the

36

coach's body. The leather cover of the luggage boot at the rear of the coach had been slashed open, the light brown edges where a knife had cut through three or four shades lighter than the cover's weathered surface.

Along the bottom edge of the wrecked vehicle, a horse's four hooves were sticking out. Now Longarm could understand why the stage lay at such an awkward angle. When it overturned during its plunge into the arroyo the horse had fallen first, dragging the coach with it. As it plunged down, the momentum of the stagecoach had caused it to turn over and it had landed on top of the horse, crushing its rib cage and quite likely breaking its neck.

"Well, now, old son, there've been plenty of runaways that've smashed up buggies and suchlike rigs, but this might be the first time that a runaway carriage ever smashed the horse that was pulling it," he muttered. His words sounded strangely loud in the still air. "And I guess the driver and passengers, if he had any, must've had to make it on shank's mare the rest of the way they were going."

He began searching the ground for footprints, but the baked soil of the arroyo's bottom was crusted hard. There were a few scuffed patches that he quickly identified as hoofprints, but no bootprints were visible on the hard-baked soil. However, if his remark did nothing else, it reminded him that he'd need to make a more detailed examination of the wrecked stage.

Selecting the sturdiest sapling a little distance away from the rim of the arroyo, he tethered the livery horse. Then, lifting his Winchester from its saddle scabbard he picked his way along the rim of the arroyo until he came to a spot where he could slide down easily. He walked

37

back along the valley floor to the wrecked stage.

At closer range, it was easy for Longarm to deduce what must have taken place, but he had no idea why the stage should have left the road at all; discovering the reason would have to wait. Climbing up on the vehicle's side, he looked through the open door. The interior of the stagecoach was empty and there was no clue that would tell whether it had been carrying passengers. He slid and crawled from the door to the driver's seat, but again there was nothing that even hinted at the fate of the man who'd been handling the reins.

Jumping from the body of the stage to the arroyo floor, Longarm walked slowly around to look at its slanting top. The first thing that caught his eye was the gleam of white bones from the spine and upper ribs of the dead horse, while the odor of soured blood invaded his nostrils. Coyote tracks were thick all around this side of the wreck, and as Longarm was about to turn away from the stench he glimpsed the print of a boot sole in the same area. It overlay the paw marks.

"Well, old son," Longarm said in the stillness of the arroyo, "looks like the fellow that potshot at you was noseying around down here when he seen you or heard you riding up. Now, he didn't have no idea who you was or why you was heading this way, so why in tunket would he be so all-fired trigger-happy?"

Turning away from the coach, Longarm began walking in slow zigzags up the arroyo floor, away from the wrecked stagecoach. He'd covered only a few yards of the area when he smelled an odor alien to the clean air of the high desert. For a moment he did not believe the message his sense of smell was sending him, then he saw the glint of metal a few yards distant and hurried to it. A gallon-sized kerosene can that had been hidden by a clump of saplings stood beside a spade that lay on the ground.

Neither of these held his attention for more than a moment, for when he lifted his eyes to glance beyond them he saw for the first time the heaped oblongs of freshly turned soil that could be only one thing: a pair of freshly covered graves.

Chapter 4

"Whoever held up that stage sure wasn't going to leave no witnesses," Longarm muttered. "Nor no stagecoach, neither, judging by that can of kerosene. And it looks like you're going to have to do a little digging to find out why, old son."

For a moment Longarm did not move. Then he began walking slowly toward the mounded oblongs of raw dirt. With the position of the graves fixed in his mind, he did not look at them again. Instead, he studied the sparsely covered ground around them, looking for footprints that now or later might give him a lead to finding the person or persons who'd dug the graves. His examination was quick but thorough, and totally unproductive.

There were a few scuffed areas in the hard-baked soil around the mounds, but the dry dirt clods that remained on the surface after the graves had been filled had not kept their shape as moist soil does. They had crumbled to small dusty bits, none of them bigger than a man's thumb. They gave many signs of the grave digger's movements, but retained no identifiable prints of his boot soles.

"Well, old son, just standing here looking at a pair of graves ain't going to help you a whole lot," Longarm told himself as he touched a match to the fresh cigar he'd taken out while he was studying the area around the graves. "So even if it ain't a real nice job, you better go get that shovel and do a mite of uncovering."

Having made his decision, Longarm wasted no more time. He returned to the spot where he'd found the shovel and kerosene can, picked up the shovel and re-turned to the graves. Working carefully, never thrusting the sharp edge of the spade deep enough to slice into the body he was sure the grave held, he began removing the dirt from the end of one of them. The job of lifting out the dry sandy soil was not difficult, and only a short time passed before the careful scraping of his shovel had exposed the rounded peak of a hat's crown.

Pushing the loose dirt aside now rather than digging, Longarm had the hat fully exposed after a few more minutes of careful work. He bent down to remove it. The eyes of the dead man stared up glassily from a tanned and weatherbeaten face. His eyes were open, his lips distorted, gaping in the frozen rictus of death. A few strands of bloodstained grey hair straggled across his balding forehead, almost hiding the bullet hole in one side of his head. A thick grey mustache almost con-cealed his upper lip. His jaw sagged, his mouth gaping open to show a snaggle of yellowed teeth.

Longarm had not expected to recognize the dead

man, and he was not disappointed. For a few moments he studied the face of the corpse, long enough to fix it firmly in his memory. Then he replaced the hat, moved to the second grave, and within a few minutes had un-covered the head and shoulders of its occupant. Again, the dead man's hat had been placed over his face.

When he lifted the hat Longarm saw a younger man than the one he'd just been inspecting. He placed the man's age as being in the middle or late twenties. He had a full shock of wiry coal-black hair and his cheeks and jaws were covered by a thick stubble of black whiskers. His death-glazed eyes were dark brown, his eyebrows bushy, his cheekbones high. There was no sign of a bullet wound, but the blot of red that tinged the bottom of his gaping collar was the only clue Longarm needed to deduce that a chest shot had killed him.

"Well, now," Longarm said aloud after he'd risen to his feet and puffed fresh life into his dying cigar, "looks like you got a little more to go on now. You can cross that stagecoach driver from Lordsborough off your list of suspects, since that's likely him staring into his hat in that first grave. But that don't mean so much when you consider there's a whole townful of suspects up ahead. And this can't be the stage Billy sent you after. This one was hit too recently, and was likely the one you'd have been on if you'd gotten to Lordsborough a day earlier. Looks like you're just going to have to eat this apple one bite at a time."

Replacing the second dead man's hat, Longarm picked up the shovel and scraped the dirt he'd removed back over the graves. He tilted the can of kerosene on its side and watched the inflammable liquid as it gurgled out to form a smelly wet pool that was quickly absorbed by the dry thirsty earth. When the flow stopped he upended the can to drain it completely, then with a final look at the graves and the wrecked stagecoach, he mounted up and started up the long slope leading to the trail.

A night on the raw featureless desert had done nothing to improve Longarm's temper. The time he'd spent investigating the arroyo had added to the dragging weariness of the livery horse and had thrown his schedule out of kilter. When the horse had started stumbling over the deep ruts in the trail, he'd been forced to stop short of his planned destination and bed down a few yards away from the trace of a road and spend the night on the desert.

He was still feeling short of sleep. A dozen times during the long hours of moonless gloom he'd been awakened when he'd shifted position in his light slumber. Longarm's involuntary movements had created gaps that allowed the chilly desert wind to penetrate his bedroll and awaken him with its icy exploring trickles. Both supper and breakfast had come from the emergency rations of beef jerky and parched corn in his saddlebags, so he was hungry as well as sleepy.

"Old son," he muttered as he focused his attention on the scatter of buildings that had appeared almost like magic to break the flat horizon, "this might not be the first time you've been glad to get to a stopping place, but it's sure the first time ever that the place you were glad to see had such a downright unhappy name. Because unless you're a day late and a dollar short, them buildings up ahead can't be anyplace but that town called Death."

While his tiring horse plodded on ahead, Longarm watched the town take shape. In the fashion of a few small unplanned settlements in the west, the town was not laid out in neat squares between straight streets. It seemed to have no beginning and no end.

As Longarm drew closer to town a house became visible, then another, the two widely separated and facing at entirely different angles. A short time later other houses appeared, some close, some far. There were a few places where all the houses of a cluster stood neatly aligned in a straight row and all facing in the same direction, but these were the exceptions.

Only a few of the streets on which the houses stood were fairly wide and straight, with conventional right-angled corners at which they intersected. Most of them curved and zigzagged and came together or parted at a wide variety of angles. The streets were not wide enough nor defined well enough to justify being called streets. They were trails beaten from one small cluster of houses and buildings to another.

Taken as a whole, the little town looked as though it might have been planned by a number of children just learning to make pencil marks on paper. There were a few two-story houses or business buildings, and these rose above their neighbors like big ice floes on a calm sea, but most of the structures were small, huts or hovels rather than houses. Some were neatly painted, while others were of raw fresh lumber, or showed the greying hues of boards that have been long exposed to the pitiless desert sun.

At a distance from the town itself, one group of buildings formed an orderly and imposing array. There were three of them. Two were large double-storied structures, the other one smaller and single-storied.

All of them were built of quarry stone, and even if the hoist frame that towered from the center of the cluster had not been present, Longarm had seen enough like them to identify the buildings as being the working headquarters of a mine. A short distance from them he could now see the grey humps of slag dumps.

"Now, that's a town where a man's got to learn his way around if he don't want to get plumb lost trying to find the place he's looking for," Longarm said aloud. "But it looks big enough to have a hotel or at least a boardinghouse, and likely a saloon or two where there might even be a bottle of Maryland rye."

Encouraged by having a goal in sight after looking at the barren desert for so many miles, Longarm toed his horse to a faster pace. He'd handled enough cases and covered enough miles in desert country to know that the town was farther away than it looked. With the promise of a drink, food that wouldn't have to come out of his saddlebags, and a bed to sleep in rather than a bedroll spread on the hard-baked desert soil, he was anxious to reach his destination.

By the time he'd gotten to the first outpost of houses, the sun had dropped low enough to shine in his eyes in spite of the frequent tugs he'd given his hat brim to pull it lower. Following the uncertain winding of the road, Longarm passed by a few ramshackle hovels and came at last to a cluster of business buildings.

At close range now, he could see that these were as variegated as the houses. Some were neat, a few even showed signs that they'd been painted recently. The unpainted buildings revealed their age by the degree to which the boards had changed color from their original bright, new-sawn yellowish tan to the deep brown of maturity or the dull grey of extreme age. Longarm's cases had taken him to so many towns which were similar that he noted the differences in the houses almost unthinkingly.

Finally he saw the one word he'd been looking for on the false second-story front of a building a short distance ahead: SALOON. He reached the hitch rail in front of the oasis, dismounted, looped his horse's reins over the rail and pushed through the batwings.

Longarm saw nobody in the long narrow barroom, not even the barkeeper. Apparently the thunking of Longarm's boot heels on the scarred and battered floor could be heard in whatever back-room retreat the man had been in, for by the time Longarm had reached the stretch of mahogany, the faded red drapes near its center and behind it parted as a stubby, chunky man pushed through them.

"Howdy, stranger," he said. "Step up and I'll be glad to pour whatever you might fancy."

"Maryland rye," Longarm replied. "Tom Moore, if you've got any."

"Just happens I do," the barkeep said, nodding. He turned to the backbar and selected a bottle, wiped the dust off on his soiled white apron and picked up a shot glass before returning his attention to Longarm. As he placed bottle and glass on the bar, he went on, "Always glad to see a stranger come to town, and from that load of dust you're carrying you've been in the saddle for quite a spell."

"A pretty good while," Longarm agreed. He was filling the glass in front of him as he spoke. Before lifting his drink he fished a cigar out of his vest pocket and

47

lighted it, then took out a cartwheel and dropped it on the bar. The amenities observed, he tossed off the drink and put the glass back on the bar. The barkeep hastened to refill it.

"This one's on the house," he said. "If you're like most men that fancy good rye whiskey, you wouldn't try to walk on just one leg."

"Only when I've got to," Longarm replied. He lifted the refilled glass and contented himself with a modest sip before going on. "I ran into something back up the road a ways that I need to talk to your sheriff about. I guess you got one in town? Or a deputy, or somebody?"

"Oh, sure. The courthouse is about midway between here and the smelter. That's them big stone buildings out a ways beyond town. If you're heading for the courthouse, go on down to where Smedley's Grocery is and turn right. You'll know it when you see it, I guess."

"I guess," Longarm agreed. "One courthouse looks pretty much like the next one, I've found."

"Sure. Sheriff Blanton might not be there now, though. It's about the time of day when he heads home for a little nap and supper, before he makes a couple of rounds in the evening. But I can tell you where his house is at, if you're in a hurry."

"I ain't," Longarm answered. "Besides, I need to find me a place to stay before it gets too late. I reckon there's a hotel here?"

"Well, Angie Martin don't call it that. She's named it the Enfolding Arms, which gives a lot of strangers the idea it's a fancy house. But it's the nearest thing to a hotel as you'll find here in town. Don't serve no meals, though."

"That wouldn't make no never-mind. This Angie Martin, she'd be the landlady?"

"That's right. Nice-looking one, too."

"It sounds all right to me, so since you say it's all right, that's where I'll head. How do I get there?"

"Just turn right when you get outside and start walking, it's just a skip and a holler away."

Longarm had drained the refilled glass while the barkeep was talking. He put it back on the bar and tapped its rim with a fingertip. While the barman filled it again Longarm resumed their conversation.

"If the sheriff should happen to drop in before I catch up with him, you might mention that I'd like to visit with him for a little bit," he said. "My name's Custis Long. Deputy United States marshal outa the Denver office."

"Right pleased to make your acquaintance, Marshal. I'm Todie Moore."

Longarm nodded in recognition of the introduction, then said, "I guess you'd know something about that stagecoach from Lordsborough that never has pulled into town?"

"Seeing as you're a stranger to these parts, maybe I better tell you something about that stagecoach, Marshal Long. And when you get talking to the sheriff, he'll tell you the same thing. That damn stage ain't got a regular time to pull in or to pull out. It comes and it goes the way that suits old Jason Cheever. He owns the rig and he runs it just about any damn way he pleases."

Longarm quickly changed his mind about discussing

49

the stage to any greater extent than was necessary. Instead he asked, "Then nobody'd be apt to worry if it was a day or two late?"

"I'll tell you this," Todie Moore replied. "That damn stage comes in late a lot more times than it does early."

"Just what would you call late?" Longarm frowned.

"I'd say a day or two. Once in a while three."

"And it just runs between here and Lordsborough?"

"Oh, no. Death, here, is about in the middle of the run the stage makes. Old Jason's got the franchise to run from Tucson to Lordsborough. That is, the Southern Pacific's got the franchise, but they're a long ways from being ready to lay track, so they made a deal with Jason for him to fill in the gap with his stage."

"Well, now, that answers a lot of questions that I ain't had time to ask yet," Longarm said. "I thank you kindly for the information, and now I'll be moseying along."

Scraping his change off the bar into his hand, Longarm went back to the street and levered himself into the saddle. He let the tired animal set its own pace and it moved slowly along the unpaved street. He'd gone past three or four nondescript buildings when he saw the Enfolding Arms. Though the low-slung two-story building itself was one of the many he'd seen in Death that needed paint and a few new shingles, he pulled his horse up at its hitch rail and went inside.

Longarm found himself in a small entry not large enough to be described as a room. The cubicle held only a little square table, on which lay an open registration ledger. He'd just bent forward to look at the exposed pages when a light tattoo of footsteps sounded in the hall and a woman came into the entry.

She did not look either old or young, but seemed poised on the edge between both. A towel was wrapped around her head, her dress was a nondescript grey. Her lightly tanned face bore no trace of rouge or powder, nor had she smeared her mouth with lip salve. Her eyes were a deep brown, and met Longarm's steadily as her full eyebrows rose questioningly.

"I imagine you're looking for a room?" she asked. "If you are, I'm Angela Martin, the landlady."

"I'll need a place to sleep tonight. If you've got one to rent, I'd likely take it," Longarm said.

"Would you like to look at it first?"

"I ain't all that finicky, ma'am. As long as you say it's all right, I'll take your word. All I want's a bed and a place where I can shave and sorta clean up. I've been on the road a spell. I guess you can tell that."

"You're not the first traveler who's stopped here," she said with a smile. "And I don't judge men like you at first look."

"Then I guess you got a room vacant I can rent?"

"Of course. There aren't very many people who come here these days. And you'll find that I keep a nice clean rooming house," she went on. "I don't hold with bedbugs or fleas or cockroaches. Rats or mice, either. Or drunk renters. If you want the room, it'll be fifty cents a day, one day free if you take it by the week. I'll see that you get a clean bath towel and washrag every week, and I'll haul your water from the kitchen. As long as you don't raise any sort of ruckus, what you do is your own business."

51

"Maybe I better tell you, Miss Martin, I'm a deputy U.S. marshal and I'm here on a case. My name's Long, Custis Long. I might be going out or coming in at night when your other roomers are sleeping, but I'll try to be real quiet when I'm traipsing up and down the hall."

"I doubt that you'll bother anybody, Marshal Long," she replied. "Now, if you'd like to look at the room before you pay me tonight's rent—"

"I'll likely be here for three or four days, maybe more," Longarm broke in. He dug into his trouser pocket. Taking out three cartwheels, he dropped them into her hand as he went on, "I can't be sure till I've noseyed around a little bit. But I'll be glad to pay you for a week, just in case."

"Whatever's most convenient for you, Marshal Long," Angela Martin offered. She dropped the money into her apron pocket as she said, "Now, if you'll follow me, I'll show you your room and the conveniences."

Longarm followed her down the hall, where she opened a door near its end. "Your room," she said.

Peering over her shoulder, Longarm gave the room a quick glance. It held a bed, chair, and a small combination bureau-washstand. He nodded as he told her, "It'll do just fine. I'll toss my gear in it right now, if it's all the same to you."

"Of course." Pointing to a closed door at the end of the corridor, she said, "And the conveniences are behind that door. If you want hot water for shaving or a bath, I'll have to get it for you from the kitchen."

"I'll get along just fine," Longarm assured her. "What I want to do right now is just stretch out and nap a spell. Then I'll clean up and go about my business."

"I'll leave you to rest, then," she said. "When you're ready to shave, just ring the call bell."

Longarm watched her go down the hall and start upstairs, then he went into his room. He did not bother to lever out of his boots, and just tossed his hat on the bedside chair and stretched out on the bed. In two minutes he was asleep.

Chapter 5

Loud angry voices from the hall outside his door woke
Longarm from a sound sleep. Almost before his eyes
were open his hand had started for his Colt—which
he'd placed on a chair at the bedside—and he was rolling out of the bed. He had to stop for a moment to recall
the direction of the door, then he reached it in two long
steps and flung it open.

In the dim light that trickled down the narrow passageway from a lamp at its opposite end he saw Angela
Martin standing in the grasp of a seedy-looking man
who held a half-full bottle of whiskey in his other hand.
She was tugging at his wrist, trying to break free.

"Suppose you let go of the lady, now," Longarm
said. He did not raise his voice, but its tone carried its
own message.

"And suppose you butt outa something that ain't

none of your business!" the man snapped, raising the bottle menacingly.

Longarm grasped the man's wrist and jerked it toward himself as he whirled into a half turn. His moves threw the other man off balance. The stranger dropped the bottle and lurched to one side, releasing his grip on Angela's wrist as he pawed the air to keep from falling. Snarling angrily, he managed to avoid tumbling and launched a swooping swing aimed at Longarm's jaw.

Longarm blocked the swing with the hand in which he held his Colt. The stranger's fist thwacked into the cold hard steel of the revolver. He yowled with pain and began trying to back away, but could not free his wrist from Longarm's iron grip. Freed now from the drunk's grasp, Angela began kicking her assailant's shins.

"Leave go of me!" the man yowled. "Just let me alone and I'll go peaceful! I wasn't meaning no harm to nobody!"

Looking at Angela, Longarm asked, "Should I turn him loose? I sure won't mind hauling him to the lockup if you say so."

"Oh, let him go," she replied. "He hasn't really done anything except spill his liquor on my floor, and I can mop that up without any trouble."

"I'll just see him to the door, then," Longarm said.

He whirled the man around and pushed him along the hall to the door. Opening it, he propelled the intruder into the street with a final shove. The drunk sprawled forward, lurching to keep from falling on his face, and began reeling down the street. Longarm stood watching him for a moment, then closed the door and went back down the long hallway.

Angela was already kneeling, wiping up the spilled

56

whiskey with the edge of her apron. She looked up at Longarm and said, "I'm sorry you were disturbed, Marshal Long, but thanks a lot for your help."

"You were holding your own pretty good from what I saw," Longarm told her. "But I hope you ain't bothered by men like him very often."

"Very seldom," she replied. "Once in a while somebody like that drunk gets the idea in his head that just because I rent rooms my company is included with the room."

"I don't reckon you'll need to worry about him coming around anymore," Longarm went on. "And maybe it's just as well I got waked up. I still got business to take care of before I turn in for the night."

"I don't lock the front door until midnight," she said. "If your business keeps you out later than that, just pull on the bell cord and I'll let you in."

"I ain't figuring to be so late getting back," he told her. "First I got to grab a bite to eat, then I'll stop in at the sheriff's office. If I don't catch him there I'll take a turn around town to see if I can run into him while he's making his rounds. If I miss him tonight, there's plenty of time to look him up tomorrow morning."

Angela nodded and returned to her work. Longarm stepped back into his room to buckle on his gun belt and holster his Colt, then moved on to the door. Outside, the heat of the day had been dispelled by a light fitful breeze. He stopped just outside the door for a moment, looking at the livery horse that stood patiently at the hitch rail, then glanced along the almost deserted street, searching for a livery stable.

None of the buildings within sight bore the sign he'd hoped to see, and the windows of most of them were dark. Swinging into the saddle, he started the horse at a slow walk along the quiet street. He'd covered only a short distance when the lamps glowing through the window of one of the stores that still remained open silhouetted the words SMEDLEY'S GROCERY.

Suddenly Longarm recalled the directions given him by the barkeep at the saloon where he'd stopped. He looked beyond the building, and a glance along the street was enough for him to identify the courthouse. Its bulk was unmistakable, and the only light he saw along the deserted street was spilling through a window at one of the building's corners. He reined the horse toward the light.

As he approached the building Longarm got an occasional glimpse of someone moving around inside the lighted room. Catching sight of a horse hitched to a rail in front of the building, he hitched his own mount beside it. The dark rectangle of a door near the building's corner was also visible now. Longarm started toward the door, and even before he reached it he saw the legend SHERIFF on its top panel. Opening the door without knocking, he stepped inside.

"Evening, stranger," the grizzled man standing beside a paper-strewn desk greeted him. "Something I can help you with?"

Longarm had already seen the badge pinned on the speaker's shirt pocket. He extended his hand as he stepped toward him, saying, "Long's my name, Sheriff. Custis Long, deputy United States marshal outa the Denver office."

"Fred Blanton," the sheriff said. "And I reckon you'd be the one they call Longarm. I heard about you from Bert Mossman, up at Bisbee."

"Sure," Longarm replied. "Me and Bert worked a case together some time back."

"And it's a case that's brought you here, I take it?"

"Now, Sheriff Blanton, you know that's the only way a man in our line gets outa the office." Longarm smiled, then his face grew sober as he went on, "There's a wild shooter running loose on the desert out east of here, Sheriff. He tried to peg me, but that's only the half of it. If you've been wondering about the stage from Lordsborough being late, it's because it won't be here at all."

"Oh, we're used to it being late," Blanton said. "It'll pull in sometime tonight, I imagine."

"Not likely," Longarm replied. "At least, not the one I stumbled onto. It's all smashed up, laying on its side on top of the horse in an arroyo about midway between here and Lordsborough. And before you ask me any more questions, I found the driver and I'd guess the shotgun messenger that'd been buried in that same arroyo."

"It's murder you're talking about, then?"

Longarm nodded. "Not any mistake about it. There were bullet holes in both of the bodies."

"You think the fellow that shot at you killed 'em?"

"Maybe. He did it before I happened by, if he did," Longarm said thoughtfully. "Coyotes had been chewing on the horse, but I've seen enough dead men to judge, and I'd say they were shot yesterday. If he had a hand in it, he'd likely just come back to bury 'em. He had a shovel, and the dirt was fresh turned. It'd figure, if he was maybe part of a holdup gang that robbed the stage, and he'd come back to burn it and had put the bodies where nobody'd be likely to stumble over 'em."

"But he got away."

59

"He was running before I wheeled off of the road to go after him. He had such a start I didn't have a chance to catch him, so I stopped and began noseying around."

"That's when you found the wreck of the stage and the bodies?" the sheriff asked.

"Like I just said," Longarm replied. "And alongside it there was a shovel and a gallon can of kerosene. It don't take much figuring to see why that hombre that shot at me was there."

"Getting rid of evidence," Blanton confirmed.

"Them bodies hadn't been there more than overnight," Longarm went on. "Stands to reason that the fellow who began sniping at me left 'em there when he turned tail and ran."

"I don't suppose you got a good look at the man who got away?"

"He was already cutting a shuck before I left the road, Sheriff Blanton. And that spade and kerosene can were the only things I saw at first. Then I noticed the graves, so I uncovered 'em enough to see who was in 'em."

"And I'm sure you didn't recognize them."

Longarm shook his head. "They weren't ripe at all, so they hadn't been buried long. There wasn't any use I could see to dig 'em out, so I just shoveled the dirt back over 'em. I gave the coach a good going over, but it was bare as Bodley's bones."

"This looks like it's turning into some kind of big case," Blanton said with a frown. "Who in hell would want to take a stagecoach and burn it up?"

"I got a pretty good idea, but we can get to that later," Longarm replied.

"Just how come you're so interested in that stagecoach, Longarm? That is, if you don't mind telling me. I suppose you know there was another stagecoach that disappeared on the way here from Lordsborough a month or so ago?"

"So I've heard."

"And we'd both be damned fools if we didn't realize there has to be some sort of connection between the one you found today and the one that vanished some time ago."

"Did you do any noseying around when that other one turned up missing?" Longarm asked.

Blanton shook his head. "What kind of work can a lawman do on a case like that? I don't need to tell you how many places there are around here where somebody could tuck it away."

"I'd imagine there's a lot more miles than people in your jurisdiction," Longarm said. "It was a pure accident that I happened to be passing by the place where that fellow was getting ready to set fire to the other one."

"If you don't mind me saying so," Blanton said, "I can't figure out how this business with the stages has anything to do with a federal case."

Longarm made a snap judgment. Then he said, "There ain't nothing real secret about why I was sent here. Some Treasury Department vouchers have turned up missing. They were supposed to go to the mine here, but they just sorta disappeared. I was sent to find whoever stole 'em."

"So that's where the stagecoaches come in," Blanton said. "The vouchers would've been put on both of them at Lordsborough."

"Don't jump to conclusions," Longarm warned. "I

don't know for sure that there were any vouchers on the stage I found."

"Well, that pretty much gives me the answer to what happened to the one that's still missing," Blanton added. "But I'm damned if I know where to start looking for it now. It's probably gone up in smoke by this time."

"You're likely right," Longarm agreed. "There's not much chance it's ever going to turn up. But them Treasury vouchers are pretty sure to. If they're like all the other ones I know about, there'll be a time limit on cashing 'em."

"I guess I don't follow you," Blanton admitted. "But I'm not used to getting mixed up in cases that come under federal jurisdiction."

"There ain't all that much to it," Longarm said. "It used to be that when somebody got a Treasury voucher they'd just tuck it away till they needed extra cash, then trot down to the bank and cash it in. But when the big money panic came along ten years or so ago, just about everybody that had a voucher ran to the nearest bank to cash it."

"I remember that there was a big panic back in the seventies," Blanton put in when Longarm paused to light one of his long thin cigars. "All of a sudden the money dried up, and everybody had a pretty tough time of it."

"And just about everybody that had a Treasury voucher went running to the nearest bank to cash it in." Longarm nodded. "There were so many of 'em that the banks and the government both came damn close to running outa cash. That's when the Treasury changed the rules. Nowadays them vouchers have got to be cashed inside of six months or turned in for new ones."

"I suppose whoever's got those stolen vouchers will know that," Blanton said thoughtfully.

"Oh, they're waiting it out right now," Longarm told him, "but whoever's behind all this has got to know exactly what they're doing. We're really getting down to cases, now. Of course, this is your territory, Sheriff. You got any guesses about who it might be?"

"Not right at the minute," Blanton replied. "Death's not a big enough town to hold a lot of hard characters. There's maybe four or five and they generally behave themselves as long as they're in my jurisdiction. All of 'em know that as long as they lay low I'll let 'em pretty much alone."

"Well, I can see why," Longarm said. "But whatever gang it was that held up them stagecoaches sure wasn't no bunch of angels."

"I'd say there's only about two places where you might look for the kind of men we've been talking about," Blanton went on after a brief thoughtful pause. "One's the OL Ranch, over in New Mexico Territory. There's a few hard cases mixed in with the hands."

"They give you trouble in town?"

"Some. Mostly around payday when the hands come in to look for the elephant and listen to the owl."

"And I'd guess the other place is the smelter?"

"I'd say it's a toss-up between the smelter and the mine. Old Baxter Smollet owns both of them. He owns the bank, too, and spends about all of his time there. Pat Howard's the smelter manager, and he's, well, I guess you'd call him Baxter's handyman, because he's got a hand in most of Baxter's pies."

"And likely the folks here in town look on Smollet as

the leading citizen?" Longarm's tone of voice showed that his question was also its own answer.

"Oh, there's not any doubt about that." Blanton smiled. "Old Baxter agrees with 'em, too."

"He'll be the first one I'll stop in on tomorrow morning, then," Longarm said. He glanced around the office, deserted except for himself and the sheriff, and went on, "I reckon you're just down here at this time of the evening to catch up on paperwork and little chores like that?"

"It's about all I can do to keep up," Blanton answered. "It seems like there's a little bit more every day than there was the day before."

"You just better be glad you ain't in a federal job," Longarm said. "Billy Vail—he's the head marshal in the office I work outa in Denver—Billy gets just about weighted down trying to keep his paperwork straight. But what I was getting at is that it's about time for me to wet my whistle and have a bite of supper. If you can take the time, I'll stand treat."

"If you put it that way, Longarm, there's nothing I'd be doing this evening that won't wait for tomorrow. I'll be real glad to join you. And I don't have a nickname like you do, but why don't you just get used to calling me Fred?"

"Sure. It's always easier in our trade to be friendly. Now soon as you're ready, I am, too."

Leaving Longarm's livery horse hitched in front of the courthouse, the two men started walking along the dark street. The star-filled sky ahead of them was broken by a half dozen glowing patches, the shine of lights from windows of the few stores and saloons that were still open.

64

"For a little town like this, you actually got quite a few places that don't close up at sundown," Longarm commented after they'd covered about half the distance toward the reflected glows.

"That's because the smelter works around the clock," Blanton replied. "They can't afford to let their furnaces cool."

"From what little I've learned kicking around mining towns on my cases, you got to have coal to run a smelter, and I don't recall there being much around this part of the country."

"There's not. But old Baxter Smollet's worked out a deal with the big smelter at Lordsborough. They've got a lot of low-grade lignite deposits in that part of New Mexico Territory, and when he sends his first-run silver up there his wagons all come back loaded with coal."

"Smollet's the big wheeler-dealer hereabouts, I gather."

Blanton nodded. "Always has been. The story is that he was driving a one-horse wagon on the way from El Paso to Tucson with a load of Mexican trade goods and the horse died right here where the town is now."

"So he stayed?"

"Well, there wasn't any way he could pull the wagon himself, and he couldn't afford to leave it. The Chiricahuas and Apaches were still pretty thick back then, so he set up a trading post in what was left over from old Fort Wallen. Called the place Death because his horse had died. He stumbled onto the silver lode not long after he'd settled in, and he's been here ever since."

"He must be getting up in years by now," Longarm commented.

"Nobody knows how old he really is, and he's not telling. Seems to be—"

A shot cracked from the darkness behind them. The slug whistled inches above their heads and splinters flew from the wooden wall of the closed store they were passing.

Both Longarm and Blanton hit the dirt, clawing out their pistols as they dropped. The invisible sniper's weapon cracked for a second time. The bullet sang well above them and spatted as had the first into the front wall of the closed store.

This time Longarm had glimpsed the spurt of muzzle blast. He let off an answering round. An unaimed snapshot, the lead from his Colt was swallowed by the night's gloom.

"Damned if I ain't tired of being shot at by somebody I can't see!" he exclaimed as his eyes searched the darkness.

"You mean that somebody's tried to shoot you since you got here?" the sheriff asked.

"Not here in town. I was thinking about out on the desert while I was on the way here from Lordsborough."

"Could the fellow who tried to get you then have followed you into town?"

"He could've," Longarm told him. "But after what I saw out where that stage was wrecked I kept my eyes peeled pretty good all the rest of the way in. If he got anyplace close to me, then he's a lot better at dodging than I am at seeing."

While they talked, neither Longarm nor Blanton took their eyes off the area from which the shots had come. As unlikely as it was that they'd be able to see anyone moving in the darkness, or that anyone could see them in the deep shadow of the store building, they held their positions for several minutes.

At last Longarm said, "Whoever that sniper was has probably given up by now."

"From what I've learned myself since I pinned on my badge, I think you're right," Blanton replied.

"Then let's go on to the saloon and get that drink," Longarm suggested. "And after we've chinned a little bit, I'll be about ready to go to bed. Anything I miss asking you tonight I'll catch up on tomorrow."

Chapter 6

Whether Longarm was in his own bed in Denver or a strange one in which he'd never slept before, his awakening always followed the same pattern. When the gloom of his room gave way to a dim yellowed glow created by the rising sun's light creeping through the shade of his rented room's lone window, he opened his eyes. Even before blinking them the first time in the dimness, his mind began to work, and on this morning he began at once to wonder about the identity of the mysterious sniper who'd fired last night's shots.

"There's always a chance it was some crook you nabbed someplace else, maybe way on back," he told himself as he groped for his vest and took out his first cigar of the day.

Longarm shook his head unhappily when he realized that in the rush of events that had caught him up since his arrival he'd neglected to buy a bottle of Maryland rye for his morning eye-opener. Reaching for his clothes, he dressed quickly while his mind was still absorbed in trying to recall the names of some of the crooks he'd arrested and who might by now have served out their prison terms, but the very length of his mental list discouraged him.

"There just ain't no way to recall all of 'em," he told himself at last. "But it sure could be somebody that'd served his time and been let go free. It's been that way before, and it'll likely go on being that way till you take off your badge.

"But it ain't likely to happen in a little place like this, or on a street that's darker than the inside of a bear's belly." His thoughts ran on after he'd flicked a thumbnail over a match head and lighted the cigar. As he quickly completed dressing for the day, he said, "Chances are it was the same fellow that tried to bring you down when you stopped off at that arroyo where the stagecoach and them bodies had been hidden. And if that's the case, it means he trailed after you, or maybe his hangout's someplace close by."

While engaged in his thoughts, Longarm had picked up the pitcher that stood on the nightstand. There was no need to look in it, as the vessel's weight told him it was empty. He went down the hall to the kitchen and pulled the door open. Angela Martin was sitting at the oilcloth-covered table, an empty plate pushed away from her, a cup of coffee in her hand.

"Oh, my!" she exclaimed. "I'm sorry, Marshal Long. After the little run-in with that drunk yesterday evening, I'm afraid I forgot to fill the pitcher in your room."

"Now, that don't make no never-mind," Longarm assured her. "But I slept a mite later than I generally do.

And last night me and Sheriff Blanton had a little brush with somebody we never did get a good look at and had to dive for the dust."

"Goodness!" Angela frowned. "I hope you got whoever was shooting at you!"

"Neither one of us was hit, but the scoundrel that tried to cut us down got away free and clear. Then after we'd had a drink or two, I was a mite sleepy when I got back here, so I just plopped into bed without bothering to wash up."

"Well, hand me your pitcher and I'll go fill it. The water barrel's just outside the door over there."

"Now, it ain't no use in you getting up. Go on and finish your coffee while I dip up a pitcher of water."

Angela opened her mouth as though to protest, but said nothing as she nodded. Longarm stepped out to the water barrel and dipped until the pitcher was almost full, then reentered the kitchen. Angela was standing beside the stove, an egg sizzling in a skillet while she was breaking another one into the pan.

"You're not going out of here without breakfast," she said, turning to Longarm. "Just sit down at the table and pour yourself a cup of coffee while these eggs cook."

"Well, that's real thoughtful of you, ma'am," he told her. "But when I rented my room yesterday I got the impression meals weren't included."

"It's just, well, call it a thank-you for being so helpful with that unpleasant drunk man yesterday."

"Why, I didn't do anything special," Longarm said as he settled into one of the chairs beside the table.

"You might not call it special, Marshal Long, but I do," Angela replied. "You helped me when I needed a man's firm hand, and that's what counts."

While she was talking, Angela was sliding the sizzling eggs onto a plate. She placed them in front of Longarm and turned back to the stove long enough to open the oven and remove a smaller plate holding two biscuits.

"Now," she told him, "put something into your stomach before you start your day's work, whatever it may be. I don't have the slightest idea what would bring a United States marshal to a little town like this."

"There ain't anything secret about why I'm here," Longarm said after he'd swallowed his first bite. "I imagine you've heard about the wrecked stagecoach and a couple of bodies that I found in an arroyo between here and Lordsborough?"

"This morning at the grocery store I heard about them being found, but I didn't know it was you who discovered them." A puzzled frown was forming on her face as she spoke. She went on, "But that was only yesterday or the day before! You couldn't've had time to get here from—Denver, didn't you say when you rented the room yesterday?"

Longarm nodded. "I started out from Denver, all right. That's my headquarters, and it's taken me three days or thereabouts to get to Death. I just stumbled onto that stagecoach while I was on the road here."

"You've been traveling for quite a while, then."

"Oh, I'm pretty much used to it."

"And I realize now that it wasn't the stagecoach being robbed that brought you here, if you just happened to see the stage on your way to Death."

"That was just an accident. I was sent here because there's some U.S. Treasury vouchers that've disappeared. Far as the Treasury folks can tell, they disap-

72

peared someplace between Lordsborough and Death."

"I— I guess I don't understand what a Treasury voucher is." Angela frowned.

"Why, a voucher's nothing but a check from the government. If the Treasury Department has to pay out a whole lot of money, like they do for a shipment of silver ingots from Mr. Smollet's mine, the mint in Denver just sends him a voucher for whatever the silver costs 'em. It's just the same as cash money, except that it saves a lot of bookkeeping at the mint in Denver and the Treasury office back in Washington."

"If it's money for that nasty Baxter Smollet, I hope he never gets it, then!" Angela exclaimed angrily.

"Well, now!" Longarm said. "You got something against him?"

"I—" Angela stopped short. Then in a calmer voice she went on, "Yes, I'll have to admit it to you. I do have a grudge against Baxter Smollet."

"You mind telling me why?"

Angela hesitated only for a few seconds this time before continuing. A small angry frown formed on her face as she said, "When I decided to buy this house I didn't have quite enough cash. I went to Mr. Smollet's bank to ask him about taking out a loan for the amount I was short. He, well, he said the only way I could get a loan from his bank was if I'd be—well, he told me I'd have to be his fancy woman for a while."

"He just came right out with it?"

"Without wasting a word. Right then, I stood up and walked out. Since that day I've never set foot in his bank."

"And I can see you must've got the money by yourself."

73

"I certainly did. I went to Tucson and sold some jewelry that I treasured very dearly, and I found a bank there that would make me a loan—which I've paid off, by the way—so I got my house without Mr. Smollet's help."

"And from the looks of things you've done real well with it," Longarm said.

"I'm a long way from getting rich, but I'm satisfied. I'm my own boss, I don't owe anybody a penny, and, well, I guess that's all a person has a right to ask from life."

By eating during the pauses in their conversation, Longarm had found time to finish the breakfast Angela had prepared for him. He stood up. "I do thank you for my breakfast," he said. "Now I got to get moving. And even if you don't like Baxter Smollet, I got to go to his bank and talk to him a while, because he's the one that the missing vouchers belong to."

Pausing only long enough to toss his saddlebags over his shoulder, Longarm started along the street, heading for the square blocky courthouse. When he and Sheriff Blanton had parted the night before, Blanton had insisted on taking Longarm's livery horse to the county stable.

"It's closer than either of the liveries to where you're staying, and it won't cost you a dime," the sheriff had said. "Besides, it's a courtesy we offer any visiting lawman, not that there's all that many who stop off here."

Longarm stuck his head into the door of the sheriff's office when he reached the courthouse, but Blanton was not there.

"He oughta get here pretty soon," the deputy on desk

duty told Longarm. "But if you need your nag, just tell the stableman to get it saddled."

"Well, I ain't aiming to cover an awful lot of ground this morning," Longarm said, "I only have to go to the bank right now. But if I take a notion to nosey around, I figure I'm better off with a horse than without one."

So Longarm hunted down the livery, retrieved his horse, and rode the short distance to the ornate cut-stone building that housed the bank and went inside. There were no waiting lines at either of the teller windows. When he asked for Baxter Smollet at the nearest of them, the teller shook his head.

"Mr. Smollet doesn't talk to just anybody and everybody that comes in off the street," he said. "Not unless you've got an appointment, and I don't see any names on his caller list."

While the teller was talking Longarm had taken out his wallet. He flipped it open to show his badge as he said, "I got a notion he'll want to talk with me about some Treasury vouchers that's turned up missing."

Without changing his expression, the teller pointed toward a door at the back of the bank's lobby. With a nod of thanks, Longarm walked through the lobby to the door the man had indicated and tapped on its frosted glass panel.

"All right, come in!" a voice called from the room beyond.

In spite of himself, Longarm almost lost his usually impassive poker face when he got his first look at the man ensconced in the high-backed oversized leather swivel chair behind the gleaming polished desk that filled most of the small room.

Bright morning sunlight shining through the barred

window behind his chair gleamed from a totally bald head and threw the man's face into shadow. Then as Longarm's eyes adjusted to the glare from the unshaded window, he saw that the face of the chair's occupant was a sagging mass of deep overlapping wrinkles. They seemed to be competing for space, crisscrossing from his temples down his cheeks to a series of drooping triple chin wattles that almost completely concealed his starched white collar and black bow tie. Even his eyelids were wrinkled, and they were closed to mere slits that showed pupils of icy blue.

"Well?" the man growled. "Who the hell are you and why'd you knock on my door?"

"I figured it'd be sorta polite to knock instead of just busting in," Longarm answered. "Custis Long's my name, Mr. Smollet. Deputy United States marshal outa the Denver office. I came here to see you about some Treasury vouchers that's turned up missing."

"Hmph!" Smollet grunted. "I didn't have anything to do with losing 'em. Don't see why I need to do anything about getting 'em back, either. That's your job. I look for you to take care of it."

"Oh, I ain't going to argue about that," Longarm replied. "Except I figure that I'm due a little bit of help. You own this bank and the mine the silver came out of. You live here and know the country better than I do. If you got any ideas about what could've happened to the missing vouchers, I'd like to hear about 'em."

"I don't," the banker snapped. "All I know is that the quarter of a million dollars those vouchers represent is money that's due me, money I can use right now. And I want them on my desk as quick as you can put them there."

"Now, that's plumb outa my reach," Longarm told him. "But I was told in Denver that there'd be new ones sent you."

"What you're saying is that I can look for them when I get them," Smollet grunted sourly. "And I don't suppose that'll be any time soon. Now, if you want to ask any more questions, Marshal Long, get hold of my manager."

"Has he got an office here in the bank?"

As though Longarm had not spoken, Smollet went on, "If you'd had sense enough, you'd've gone to him instead of bothering me. His name's Patrick Howard. You'll likely find him out at the mine. He spends more time there than he does here. Just close the door behind you when you go out. I don't like for people in the lobby to be gaping at me."

Smollet closed his eyes and leaned back in his chair. Longarm could see that he'd be getting no more information or even any more attention from the crusty banker. He left, closing the door, and went through the lobby to the man at the window where he'd first stopped.

"I reckon you'd know if Mr. Howard's around?" he asked.

"Haven't seen him all day," the teller replied. "As a matter of fact, I haven't seen him for close to a week. But chances are you'll find him out at the mine, or maybe the smelter. They're right together on the road southeast of town, and that's where he is most of the time."

"So Mr. Smollet said. I just figured to make sure. Thanks for telling me where to look."

Outside, the dusty street showed no greater signs of

activity than Longarm had observed earlier in the day. He mounted and reined his horse onto the rutted road that led to the tall rising stacks he'd already identified as Smollet's smelter. Judging by its stacks, it was a good three miles distant.

Even though he'd gotten an early start and the day was only past midmorning, the sun was beating down on the barren land. A small breath of ground heat competed with the warmer air, which even now seemed to be pushing its heavy heat downward.

When he at last topped the last rise leading to the smelter, Longarm looked down into a broad valley. The stacks he'd seen from town rose from the valley floor and cut the line of the horizon. As he drew closer and could make out details he saw that the smelter was a closely huddled group of three sheet-iron-covered buildings with one of the tall brick stacks rising above each of them.

Threads of smoke or fumes trickled from the stacks and dissipated in the clear sunny air. On the raw ground between the buildings narrow sets of tracks formed a maze of shining steel. The tracks ran across the land in front of the buildings to the high wall of the valley, where three great black blobs of darkness broke its red-brown wall. At first glance Longarm was puzzled by the seemingly aimless spread of the rails, but as he studied the maze they formed on the floor stretching from the bluffs he realized that the rails formed a pattern. Their paths had been carefully designed to allow any of the ore carts to be moved to any of the mine shafts as well as to any of the three smelter buildings.

Though there was no one visible on the floor of the big excavation, it was readily apparent that men must be working in both the smelter buildings and the shafts. Rumbling noises of some kind of engine and harsh metallic clatterings were coming from the buildings.

"Well, now, old son," Longarm muttered as he took out a fresh cheroot and lighted it without interrupting his study of the scene, "looks like that Baxter Smollet is a right smart fellow if he's the one that put all this together. Too bad he ain't as polite as he is smart."

Longarm broke off his soliloquy when he saw a small group of men emerging from one of the smelter buildings. There were four men in the party. They stopped between the buildings and the yawning black mouths of the mine shafts. Longarm was too far away to hear what they were saying, and he toed his horse ahead.

Absorbed in their discussion, which involved much arm waving and gesticulating, the men beside the smelter buildings did not notice Longarm until they began to break up, indicating that their heated discussion was at an end. By this time, Longarm was within hailing distance.

"Hello, there!" he called. The noises from the buildings were much louder now and Longarm raised his voice to a shout as he went on, "My name's Long, Custis Long. Deputy United States marshal outa the Denver office. I came out here to talk to a man by the name of Pat Howard. Can one of you gents tell me where I might start looking for him?"

"You don't need to start looking," one of the quartet volunteered, stepping closer to Longarm. "I'm Pat Howard."

"Well, then, I'll just keep my saddle warm while

you're winding up your confab," Longarm said. "Then me and you can talk a few minutes."

"No need for you to wait," Howard replied. "We've finished our business. Light and come on over, and you can tell me what's brought you here, even if I do have a pretty good idea what's on your mind."

While Longarm dismounted and walked up to Howard the other men drifted away. As he approached the waiting man, Longarm took stock of him. Pat Howard was a tall man, topping Longarm's towering frame. His face was thin and pale in contrast to Longarm's tan. Under needle-thin eyebrows his eyes were a light, almost colorless blue. In spite of the day's warmth, he wore tight-fitting gloves of thin deerskin.

"I'd imagine you're on the trail of those missing Treasury vouchers," Howard said as Longarm stopped in front of him. "And I hope you'll have better luck than I've had trying to run 'em down. All I know is that they've disappeared."

"Along with two stagecoaches," Longarm added. "Except that I stumbled onto one of them coaches on the way here from Lordsborough. Or ain't you heard about that yet?"

Howard shook his head. "No. But I've been bunking down out here at the mine for the last several nights. We've had some trouble with the vanners."

"You're talking over my head now," Longarm said. "But I reckon what you're talking about has something to do with your smelter here?"

"It's why the smelter's had to shut down for a few days," Howard explained. "We don't do a full smelt, there's not enough water here. We just run the raw ore through the crushers and then pass it over the vanners.

80

It's the vanners we were having trouble with, but they're back in operation now."

"Hold on, now," Longarm broke in. "You're still talking about things I don't understand."

"It'll be easier to show you than try to tell you," Howard said. "Come on inside with me, and I'll show you, if you've got the time to spare."

"If I didn't have time, I'd make some," Longarm replied. "You go ahead and I'll be right alongside you."

Chapter 7

Longarm followed Howard into the building. The passageway they entered was narrow and the banging noises that had reached his ears while outside now sounded like a series of reports from a battery of small cannons. The air swiftly grew warmer and after a few steps Longarm began to feel the floor vibrating under his feet. The sensation was a bit disconcerting, and he moved more and more carefully as the floor's shivering became constant.

Soon the two-inch-thick planks underfoot began rising and falling, but by now Longarm was getting accustomed to the constant movement. He strode a bit faster to catch up with Howard, who'd slowed down and was looking back. Beyond the point where the mine superintendent stood a fine dust filled the air, its motes dancing in the light cast by big coal-oil lanterns suspended from the ceiling of the windowless building.

When he was only a step or two from Howard, the

wall on Longarm's right side ended and for the first time he could look beyond it and get a full view of the building's dimly lighted interior. Along its entire width a series of eight or ten man-high metal drums or rollers were suspended on sturdy steel rails. The big cylinders were rotating slowly above a moving belt.

Rocks and rock-studded clods of earth were being moved by the belt's slow steady advance. The clods grew progressively smaller as they traveled from one roller to the next. Men wielding long metal rods stood beside each drum and prodded at the bigger rocks that piled up against the drums and resisted being crushed by them.

Studying the moving belt and cylinders as he walked slowly beside them, Longarm saw that the bottom of each drum under which the belt moved was set to be just a bit lower than the last. The poking and prodding of the workmen along the line of the big cylinders combined with the steady relentless pressure of the rollers soon reduced even the biggest stones and clods to loose dirt and pebbles.

This residue dropped to a second belt that also moved steadily along, but the second belt ran at right angles to the first. It carried the crushed ore through an opening in the side of the building.

"I guess you can figure out what this is," Howard said to Longarm. He raised his voice to a shout to make himself heard above the constant rumbling roar.

"I can see that them rollers—except you called 'em crushers—do a fast job of smashing up them rocks pretty good," Longarm shouted in reply. "A lot faster than a whole bunch of men swinging sledgehammers could do. And I reckon the reason you smash 'em this way is to get the silver ore loose from the rocks and dirt."

"Exactly," Howard confirmed. He pointed to the end

84

of the building where the second belt was moving the pulverized mixture of loose earth and crushed stone through an opening in the wall, and said, "Now come take a look at the vanners. They're in the other building."

Howard started along the narrow planked walkway beside the moving belt, leading Longarm through a door which opened onto a well-trodden walkway that led to the second building. Even before reaching the door of the other building Longarm's ears were assaulted by a high-pitched whining noise. It grew louder when Howard opened the door and was louder still when they entered the building.

When his long step took him through the door behind his guide and Longarm stood with both feet on the walkway that ran along the walls of the high-ceilinged shedlike structure, he looked involuntarily for a post to hold on to. The walkway was shuddering underfoot and a huge fan set into the wall a few feet ahead was creating a steady current of hot desert air that swept like a dust-filled gale through the cavernous building. Howard turned to look at him and smiled.

"Don't worry about the wind or about the walk throwing you," he said. "In a minute or so you'll get used to it."

"I ain't so sure about that," Longarm replied. "This damn floor's enough to make a man giddy as a saloon whore! And that wind don't help none, either. What makes it shiver like this?"

"You saw the ore that'd passed through the crushers, all mixed up with chunks of rock." Howard indicated the small quivering platforms that stood in a long line across the floor. "It lands on these vanners and they shake the mix up so the fan can blow away the light loose dirt."

"And leave the pay dirt?"

Howard nodded. "I'm sure you know that silver ore's heavy. It stays on the vanners. So do the little specks of gold that're mixed up with the silver sometimes. There'll be a crew come in here pretty soon, they work once every hour or so. It's their job to collect the ore that's on the vanners now."

"Well, I reckon it all makes sense," Longarm admitted. "I guess after you get the ore all gathered up you melt it and cast it into bars?"

"It's not ready to be melted when it leaves here," Howard answered. "There's still too much rock mixed up with the ore. And it—" He broke off as a half dozen naked men filed in through the door leading from the building that housed the crushers. Then he went on, "Let's go outside where it'll be easier to talk and where we won't be in the way while these men collect the ore."

"It ain't none of my business," Longarm said as he and Howard emerged into the warm, still, outdoor air, "but how come that bunch was all bare-ass naked?"

"So they won't have any pockets," Howard said. "Every batch of crushed ore that goes over the vanners leaves a few loose silver nuggets on the belt, and sometimes a chip or two of raw gold as well. There's only one way to keep the men on that job from stealing those pure nuggets, and that's to make 'em work naked."

"Well, I thought I'd run across just about everything there is to do with stealing," Longarm said as he pulled a cigar from his pocket and touched a match to it. "But I got to admit, this is the first time I ever ran into a job where a bunch of men were working in their birthday suits just so they wouldn't have a place to hide whatever they'd steal."

"It's simple and it works." Howard smiled. "We did have a little trouble at first, but the hands got used to it."

"Now what was it you were going to say about melting down the ore?" Longarm asked.

"I wish it was that easy," Howard answered, his voice rueful. "You're right about one thing, though, melting—it used to be called smelting—is the last step. That's when the cleaned ore goes into the amalgamating pans to get the rest of the impurities out and then to the settling pans where the pure metal works its way down to the bottom. That's when it's ready to be collected and melted into bars."

"I figured that other building was where you did that." Longarm frowned.

"It used to be," Howard replied. "But that was before the water dried up."

"Nobody mentioned to me before now that water was so hard to come by."

"It wasn't until about two or three years ago. The springs dried up and died, the level of the San Pedro River went down and, well, all at once the country was dry."

"It's a wonder the mine's still open, then."

"Baxter Smollet's a hard man to beat, Marshal Long. He didn't want to close the mine down. There's plenty of silver ore still in the ground."

"So he came up with the answer and made a deal with that smelter in Lordsborough?"

Howard nodded and said, "We haul the vanned ore to the smelter in Lordsborough. They amalgamate it and settle it and cast it into bars."

"Ain't that a mite expensive?"

"It does cut the profit," Howard agreed. "But without

the water we need for amalgamating pans and settling pans there isn't much else we can do."

"Then you really finish up your business at Lordsborough," Longarm said thoughtfully.

"That's right," Howard said. "But you didn't come out here just to look at the mine and the smelter, Marshal Long. You said that Mr. Smollet told you to talk to me, so I suppose you've come here to find out how some of our Treasury vouchers have disappeared?"

"You hit the target square in the bull's-eye. He said you'd be the one to talk to."

"I'm afraid I don't know any more about them than he does," Howard replied, frowning as he spoke. "Unless something new's come up."

"Maybe it has, maybe it hasn't," Longarm said. "You'd know about that stagecoaches, I guess?"

"Stagecoaches?" Howard's frown deepened. "I know that one of the Lordsborough stages just dropped out of sight some time back. Are you telling me that there's another one missing now?"

"It ain't missing, but that's no fault of whoever killed the driver and another man. And whoever it was that killed 'em ran the coach into a little arroyo and was just getting ready to burn it up when I happened by and spooked him."

Howard's jaw dropped and he seemed to be struggling for words. At last he asked, "And I suppose you arrested him and he's safe in jail?"

"Not so's you'd notice. We swapped shots, but he got plumb away. I may recognize him if I see him again, though, which I don't figure's real likely. I'd guess he's cleared outa the territory by now."

"You were on your way here from Lordsborough when you had this run-in?"

Longarm nodded. "I never would've gone off the road and run across that stagecoach, except for him potshooting. The way it happened, I never did get a good close look at him."

"You said you'd recognize the fellow you traded shots with, but now you say you didn't get a good look at him," Howard pointed out. "How's that possible, Marshal Long?"

"Maybe I better put it different," Longarm replied. "There's a lot more to spotting a man than looking at his face. Now, maybe I wouldn't tumble to this fellow if I was lifting a glass in a saloon and he was standing next to me. But the minute he moved, I'd know him."

Howard still looked doubtful, but he did not follow the line of questioning. Instead, he asked, "You searched the stagecoach, I'd imagine?"

"It was bare as a baby's bottom. Not a sign of a valise or a mail pouch or anything, in the boot or in the coach."

"Then more of Mr. Smollet's vouchers are missing."

"You mean there were vouchers on that stage?" Longarm asked.

"Sure. Mr. Smollet told me he was expecting another payment that was due him. Since they get delivered here, and since I'm manager here, he tells me when to expect them," Howard said, shaking his head wearily.

"Say, something just occurred to me. Have you heard about any other stages at all dropping out of sight?"

"Like I said, Marshal, only that one. And now this second one, of course," Howard added.

"Well now, that's interesting," Longarm said slowly.

"What's on your mind, Marshal Long?" Howard asked.

89

Longarm was about to respond when he thought better of it. "Right now," he said instead, "I better just keep my guesswork to myself."

For a moment Howard said nothing. Then he nodded and said, "I take your meaning, Marshal. We'll probably run into each other again, I imagine. Right now, I'd better get on with the job Mr. Smollet's paying me to do, so if you don't have any more questions—"

"Nary a one right now," Longarm replied. "You've been right helpful. I'll bid you good-bye and let you tend to your business while I take care of mine."

Longarm let his horse set its own pace as he headed back to Death. Even after he'd reached the twisting street that led to the center of the little settlement he touched the reins only when he saw the blocky shape of the courthouse ahead, to guide his mount to its hitch rail. Swinging out of the saddle he looped the leathers over the rail and went into the sheriff's office. Its only occupant was Fred Blanton, who sat at his desk scanning some sort of legal document. He looked up as Longarm entered.

"I sorta figured you'd be stopping by before now," he said. "I take it you've been busy?"

"Yes and no, Fred," Longarm answered. "There's something going on in this place that I can smell but can't see, and it's starting to bother me."

"Bother you how?"

"That's hard to say. But I reckon there've been times when you've smelled a skunk you can't see? Or heard a rattlesnake buzzing its tail someplace close to you, but when you looked all around you couldn't locate it?"

"Oh, sure," Blanton said. "Things like that always make me stop and try to figure out the best thing to do. Is that how you feel about this case here?"

"Pretty much," Longarm agreed. "I reckon you'd know that a Treasury voucher's just like cash money, Fred. You can take one to any bank anyplace in the country and they'll give you greenbacks or hard money for it. Now, that's not to say you can cash one unless you show it's rightly yours and that you're who you say you are. But you know just like I do that any crook can always pass himself off for somebody he ain't."

"That's about the first thing I learned when I started out as a deputy sheriff," Blanton replied.

"I keep thinking back to that fellow at the arroyo that potshot me," Longarm went on. "He might be from Lordsborough, but more than likely he's got some kinda hidey-hole closer to where I ran into him. And I've also been thinking about what you told me, about how the most likely suspects would be either at that ranch you mentioned or at the mine and smelter. Now, it seems to me that even if some of the workers got greedy and decided they wanted them vouchers all to themselves, they wouldn't be stupid enough to think they could cash 'em at the bank that's run by the same man they stole 'em from. So that makes me think I oughta pay a visit to that ranch."

Blanton was silent for a moment, then he said slowly, "That would be over the line in New Mexico Territory, in that country south from Lordsborough and just east of here."

"You mean that little tit that sticks down from New Mexico Territory and by rights oughta belong to Mexico?"

"Well, who it ought to belong to's a matter of opinion. It's still sort of a no-man's-land, though. I suppose you've been there?"

"I never worked a case down there," Longarm replied. "But I know where you're talking about."

"I don't know it too well myself," the sheriff continued. "It's in New Mexico Territory and outside of my jurisdiction. My badge don't mean a thing there. But it's rough country, and the likeliest place I can think of close by where them outlaws might hole up."

"Well, you told me just about what I figured you would," Longarm said. "So I guess I better take a sashay over that way and see what I can turn up."

"By yourself, I guess?"

"There ain't but one of me," Longarm told him. "Even if my chief's joshed me a time or two about me being twins."

"It's too bad that little chunk of desert's not inside my jurisdiction," Blanton went on. "About half the hard cases that give me trouble here come off that spread."

"And you can't touch 'em, once they cross back over the line," Longarm added.

"Exactly," the sheriff agreed. "Once they're on the other side, all I can do is let 'em go."

Longarm sat silent for a moment, then said, "Like the barrel said to the box, Fred, two heads are better than one. If you can spare the time and got a real hankering to go along, I can swear you in as a temporary deputy."

"Do you want to swear me in now, or wait until the morning?" Blanton asked.

"Whichever suits you best," Longarm replied. "And if we ride outa here a little bit before daybreak we'll be across the New Mexico line before the sun gets too hot."

• • •

"There's one thing I have to say about you, Marshal Long," Angela Martin said as she opened the front door of the rooming house in response to his tug on the bellpull.

"You got my curiosity stirred up,' Longarm said. "Maybe you better tell me what that one thing is."

"You get less for your rent money than any renter I've ever had before, you're in your room so seldom." She smiled as she turned to face him after relocking the door. "I don't see how you can stay on your feet with so little sleep."

"Why, a man in my kinda work gets used to it," he said as they walked together down the hall to the door of his room. "And tonight ain't going to be much different. I'll be leaving again before daybreak."

"You mean your case is finished?"

"Not yet." Longarm was unlocking the door of his room as he went on, "And it ain't likely to be for a while. I'll only be gone maybe a couple of days. I ain't giving up my room."

"I wasn't thinking about that. I was just surprised because you've been here such a short time."

"Chances are it'll be a pretty good spell before I wind up this case. Now, that reminds me of something. I'd imagine you got a spare key to the front door, so if you want me to lock up when I go out in the morning maybe you better give it to me tonight."

"Of course I have spare keys, several of my regular lodgers use them. I'll get one from my room and bring it to you."

When Angela's light tapping sounded on the door

93

Longarm had already tossed his hat on the bureau and had shed his vest and was levering out of his boots. He'd left the door ajar, and without waiting for his reply she came in.

Longarm got to his feet and reached for the key just as Angela extended her hand to pass it to him. In the unexpected meeting of their fingers the key dropped to the floor and at the same moment both of them stooped to pick it up.

When their heads unexpectedly collided in a gentle bump, Longarm reached to grasp Angela's arm to keep her from falling. At the same time she caught hold of his wrist, and as she toppled backward pulled Longarm down with her. They fell to the floor, their legs entangling, and came to rest on the carpet with a gentle bump, Longarm sprawled on top of Angela.

Somehow Angela's free arm had gotten entrapped by his body and her hand was resting on Longarm's crotch. As they sprawled, recovering from their surprise, the involuntary pressure of her fingers closing on him brought an equally unanticipated response. Longarm felt himself beginning an erection.

"Oh, my!" Angela gasped. "I—" She stopped short and Longarm felt her fingers closing even more tightly on his swelling shaft.

"I'm sure sorry we tumbled down and wound up this way," Longarm apologized.

"It was as much my fault as yours," she answered. "And I'm glad it happened. If we hadn't fallen down together I might never have done what I'm doing now."

Hearing Angela's confession convinced Longarm to

say nothing and to let her take the initiative. He'd been in similar situations before.

Angela went on, "It's what I've been tempted to do almost from the first time I saw you. If you'll lock the door when we get up I'll show you exactly what I mean."

Chapter 8

After a few moments of floundering confusion on the floor, Longarm and Angela disentangled themselves and stood up. Longarm stepped across the room to the door and locked it. When he turned back to face her he stopped and stood staring at her. Angela was completely naked, her clothes lying in a crumpled heap around her feet. Except for the rosy tips of her budded breasts and the sparse dark curls of her pubic brush she might have been an ivory statue posed in the dimness of the low-turned lamplight.

"You'd sure make a mighty pretty picture," Longarm said as he shed his shirt, unbuckled his belt and let his breeches slide to the floor. "Except I like you better this way, where I can reach out and feel you instead of just looking."

Without shedding his balbriggans he stepped away from his heaped clothing, and now he was within Angela's reach. She grasped his wrist and pulled him to her, then released him as suddenly as she'd grabbed him. With one quick sweep of her hands she pushed Longarm's balbriggans down to his thighs. Her eyes grew wide as she saw his jutting erection.

"I knew you were a big man the first time I saw you," she told him. "But I never dreamed you'd be this big."

While Angela spoke her hands were moving to caress Longarm's rigid swollen shaft. She dropped to her knees and rubbed her soft cheeks over his firm fleshy cylinder before sliding her moist warm lips over it to engulf him.

For several moments Longarm did not disturb Angela's soft dalliance. At last he reached down and slid his hands over the jutting cherry rosettes of her generous breasts. Then he moved his strong hands to her armpits and lifted her to her feet.

Angela wasted no time. She spread her thighs and positioned his shaft, then locked her heels around his back and tightened her legs to bring him into her. Longarm took the two strides needed to reach the bed. He leaned forward, letting Angela's weight pull both of them down. They began falling, still locked in their embrace. When they landed on the bed and Angela relaxed her clasped legs, Longarm thrust and drove into her more deeply than before.

When Longarm's rigid shaft ended its sudden deep penetration Angela moaned, a bubbling prolonged sigh of pleasure from deep in her throat. Her body quivered as Longarm lunged several times with equal vigor and another long moan of pleasure escaped her lips. Now Longarm began stroking with a slow and steady rhythm. Angela quickly caught his timing and started bringing her hips up to meet the rhythm of his pounding thrusts.

"Deeper!" she gasped after a few moments. "Deeper and faster! Oh, you don't know how good you make me feel, Longarm!"

Longarm did not reply. He was concentrating on his own feelings now. Angela's hips began jerking as he kept up his long steady stroking, and for a few moments Longarm slowed his tempo. At the end of each drive he held himself motionless on her soft body until he felt her quivers fading and the upward jerks of her hips were less frantic, then he started another series of long deep lunges.

He'd just commenced driving again after a few moments spent without moving when Angela began quivering once more. Her first small moves quickly became urgent upheavals and her sighs of pleasure grew into bursts of frantic breathlessness. She locked her legs even tighter around Longarm's hips, and as he kept driving, the rolling of her hips mounted to a series of wildly twisting gyrations.

"I can't wait for you any longer," she panted. "But don't stop! Whatever you do, don't stop!"

"I ain't about to," Longarm promised without interrupting his steady tempo, "and I ain't all that far behind you."

"Together, then," she urged.

"Sure," he agreed.

Longarm began thrusting lustily once more. Angela sought his lips with hers and their questing tongues entwined again as Longarm continued his trip-hammer drives. Suddenly her body began writhing frantically beneath him. A sobbing ululation burst from her throat and she began shuddering convulsively. Longarm was

99

also peaking now. He let himself be carried on to his climax and started jetting even before Angela's cries diminished and faded into a soft satisfied panting. Then Longarm's spasms rippled away and he too lay quiet.

For a long while only the faint sounds of their breathing broke the room's silence. At last Angela said, "How long do you think you'll be gone?"

"That's sorta hard to say," Longarm replied. "Three or four days, maybe. Fred Blanton says it's most of a long day's ride to get where we're going."

"But you will be back?"

"Oh, sure, barring things I don't know nothing about yet, and won't know till we see what it's like."

"Then I guess I'll just have to wait," she sighed.

"Now, I ain't one to shortchange a lady," Longarm told her. "Just wait till we've got our second wind. Then we can start all over again. There's a pretty good spell of tonight still ahead of us."

Now that the sun had risen high enough for the wide brims of their hats to shade their eyes, Longarm and Sheriff Fred Blanton could take stock of the land ahead of them. They'd splashed across the rocky bed of the shallow San Simon River shortly before sunrise, after following the dimmest of dim trails for several hours in the predawn gloom. Two or three times they'd lost the barely visible trail in the darkness, but now with the sky bright it was easier to follow.

"Looks like that's a fork up ahead," Longarm said to his companion. He was pointing as he spoke. "You got any ideas about which way we oughta go when we get to it?"

"Just as a guess, I'd say we need to bear south,"

100

Blanton replied. "And still guessing, I'd imagine that if we turned off north on that branch we'd wind up in Lordsborough."

"You'd know that better than I do," Longarm said. "But it makes sense. And outside of this spread we're headed for, I don't imagine there's much else we'd run into."

"Not unless there's something new that I haven't heard about yet," Blanton agreed.

"Then we might as well just push ahead until we get to it," Longarm went on. "I've been doing some thinking while we've been riding, Fred. It wouldn't surprise me one bit if we ran into the jackanapes that tried to stop my clock when I ran across that wrecked stagecoach on my way to Death."

"It'd make sense," Blanton agreed. "Except for one thing."

"What's that?"

"I've known a little bit about that gang for quite some time, now. Not much, you understand, just a scrap of saloon talk here and there. I never did hear a word about them pulling a job as close to their hideout as this stagecoach case is."

"It don't take more than a mite of figuring to get the answer to that."

"Meaning what?" the sheriff prompted.

"Meaning money, Fred. You stop and figure how much them mint vouchers come to. Add up what they're worth in cold hard cash and you're talking about maybe half a million dollars, give or take a few thousand."

"That is one hell of a lot of money," Blanton agreed.

"More than fellows like you and me are likely to see as long as we live."

101

"But what good's it doing them? They're living out in this godforsaken desert country where a man can buy just about all he needs for two or three cartwheels."

"Sure," Longarm agreed, "but I never ran across an outlaw yet that didn't figure he was going to pull one more big job and quit and go live like a king in some big city. Someplace where all he's got to do is crook a finger and a pretty woman'll come running, and where he can treat himself to all sorts of fancy grub and wash it down with the best liquor money can buy."

"Now that you've mentioned it, I wouldn't mind that myself," the sheriff said, smiling.

"Oh, it dreams real good," Longarm agreed. "But I still ain't heard of a single solitary one that's done it and made it stick."

While Longarm and Sheriff Blanton talked they'd been riding steadily, their own movements furnishing the only breeze to relieve the constant heat. The glare that was reflected from the barren soil was a greater source of discomfort than the sun itself, for now the heat that the barren soil had collected through the late morning hours seeped steadily upward.

It brushed the faces of Longarm and Blanton and its heat seemed to stop and linger under their broad hat brims. The sudden ripple of extra warmth caused their eyes to water when now and then an occasional searing breath passed over their faces. At long intervals they'd lifted their canteens for a sparse sip of water, only to find their throats uncomfortably dry again before they'd put the caps back on the canteens. Neither of them commented on their discomfort, for their parched throats discouraged conversation.

After what seemed a very long time in the saddle

both of them became aware at almost the same time of a dark streak that was beginning to become visible in the shimmering heat waves that rose from the generally featureless land ahead.

Longarm turned to Blanton and said, "Now if I ain't wrong, that's—"

"Water ahead," the sheriff broke in. "I was just getting ready to point it out to you. Looks like neither one of us felt like saying anything until we were sure."

"Oh, it's water, all right, or the sign of it," Longarm said. "Even if we still got plenty in these canteens you dug out for us, it's a little bit too hot by now for it to taste real good."

"Let's just hope it's not laced too strong with alkali for us to drink a few swallows of it," Blanton said. "And then we can let these poor damn horses have a swig. They need it worse than we do."

They rode on steadily in silence until the horses began to smell the water and quickened their pace. Keeping their reins taut, Longarm and Blanton held them back for the remaining quarter of a mile. They drew to within a dozen yards of the little waterway and reined in. The tiny creek, only four or five feet wide, was so shallow that its flow was no deeper than a man's ankle. The only vegetation along its course was a thin line of sparse greenish-yellow grass.

"It ain't alkali, that's for sure," Longarm observed. "If it was that little fuzz of grass wouldn't be growing alongside it. You go ahead, I'll mind the nags."

Blanton did not object. He dismounted and drank and doused his head while Longarm held the horses a few yards away from the water. Then the men exchanged places and after Longarm had slaked his thirst and splashed a few scoops of water on his face, they led the horses to the rim of the little trickle and allowed them to drink scantily. Both men were gazing along the course of the creek through the smoke from Longarm's just-lighted cheroot when Longarm turned to the sheriff.

"You acted like you were as surprised as me to see this little trickle," he said. "At least, that's the feeling I got when we sighted it."

"I was," the sheriff agreed. "But nobody really knows this desert country around here. The old-timers say it was different twenty or thirty years ago, especially right after the war when the army was discharging a thousand bluecoats a month and the reb boys were leaving places where they used to live."

"And a lot of 'em headed west to strike gold and get rich before they got too old," Longarm put in. Though he'd splashed his face only moments before, he went again to the small creek, dipping his hat in the water and tossing it back onto his head.

"Getting back to what I started to say," Longarm went on, "we ain't got no real idea of where this place is we're looking for, or even if there is a ranch someplace around or not."

"Oh, there's a ranch all right," Blanton stated. "Even if I don't know just exactly where, I've heard enough people make remarks about it to be sure about that."

"Then don't it strike you that this little creek might just lead us to it?"

"Creeks this size pop up out of no place now and again, and the desert's as apt as not to swallow 'em before they've gone more than a couple or three miles," Blanton said, frowning. "But if you've got a notion to follow this one, I'm just as ready as you are to ride."

Mounting, they began riding slowly beside the trickling creek. They'd covered three or four miles, the declining sun more of a nuisance than ever now that it had reached a point where its rays slanted enough to creep under the brims of their hats. The creek itself did not grow or diminish, and ran almost as straight as a taut string. Against the flat featureless horizon the sky in the east began deepening in color.

"Looks like we're running outa daylight," Longarm remarked to his companion. "And it looks like I got us started on a bum steer this time, too. Far as I can tell there ain't a thing in front of us. It's still just bare as can be."

"We've been going uphill just a bit for the last several miles," Blanton told him. "But I still can't be sure where it's leading us."

"Well, I've worked a case or two here and there along the Mexican border, but this is the first time I've been along this exact part," Longarm said. "Now it'd be another thing if the Rio Grande was this far to the west, but it's way the hell and gone from where we're at now."

They rode a short distance farther and far ahead the horizon line once again became visible. Longarm and Blanton exchanged glances, as if to acknowledge it.

"Drop-off ahead," Blanton said. "Pretty good one, too, the way it looks from here."

"Makes a man feel better when he knows what to look for."

"Oh, sure."

They rode on and soon the land between them and the distant horizon began to reveal itself. The jagged rim of the drop-off was clearly visible now, and even at a distance they could tell that it was little different from the territory through which they were now passing.

"Soon as we get to that rim up in front of us there we'll know whether we've hit pay dirt or not," Longarm commented. As he spoke he was lifting himself from his saddle to stand in his stirrups.

"You won't see much farther ahead standing up that way," Blanton commented.

"Sure, I know that, but what I'm looking for right now is that little crick we crossed a ways back. It meandered away from us after we started up this slope, when we weren't paying much mind to it. I guess we're too far away to see it now."

Blanton nodded. "That's likely. We've covered a pretty good stretch of ground since we stopped to drink."

They continued their steady progress, both too tired for a great deal of conversation. A good half hour passed in virtual silence as the details of the ragged rim became more clearly visible, cutting the sky above the drop-off. Longarm, half a head taller than Blanton, was the first to see the ridge of a building's roof as it came into sight over the jagged edge of the drop-off.

"Rein in," he said the instant he was sure that he was looking at a building of some sort. "I got a hunch we've finally got to the place we've been looking for."

Reining in, still fifty or sixty yards from the saw-toothed line of the drop-off's edge, they dismounted and started walking slowly ahead. Blanton pointed to an almost house-sized boulder that rose above the jagged rim. Longarm nodded and they angled off the course they'd been following, heading now for the cover offered by the big rock formation. As they moved ahead the roof of the building became visible in greater detail.

"It's a great big ranch house," Longarm said. "No smoke coming out of either one of the chimneys, either."

"Which might mean it's too hot for a fire, granting that one of the chimneys is for the kitchen," Blanton observed. "Or it might mean there's nobody at home."

"We'll know soon enough," Longarm countered. "And just in case there is somebody around, I'd feel better if we saw whoever might be home before they catch sight of us. Let's just mosey around back of this boulder we're coming to."

Shielded by the high-rising boulder, they walked faster. The house was hidden from sight now, but beyond its edge they soon saw another roof. Its peak was long and straight.

"Barn," Blanton said succinctly. "Maybe stables with it too, looking at its size and the way the roof runs."

"Likely," Longarm agreed. "You figure this is the place we set out to find?"

"I wouldn't want to be too sure until we've found out some more, but I'd guess it is."

"There's only one way to find out any more. That's to shinny down that bluff and take a closer look."

Blanton nodded, then said, "That's what we came here for, but you're the general and I'm the soldier. You call it."

"If you wanta put it that way, the longer we dodge around up here the more likely somebody'll spot us. It don't look like there's anybody there, but if there is they might be inside. We better leave the horses here, where they'll be hidden. I don't guess it'll be too hard to scrabble down that bluff."

Delaying only long enough to drop the reins of their mounts to insure the animals would stand, Longarm and Blanton drew their rifles from the saddle scabbards and moved to the edge of the massive stone formation that was farthest from the ranch house.

As they rounded its humped rise, Longarm saw the faint pocks of boot heels in the hard earth. Wordlessly, he pointed them out to Blanton.

"We won't be the first ones to go down that bluff," he whispered. "Just give me a little bit of a start and follow along when I've got partway down."

Blanton nodded. Longarm started down the steep path, more a vestige than a well-marked trail. Digging in his boot heels to keep from sliding, he began working his way along. He'd covered a third or more of the distance when a rifle barked from the house below. The slug spattered up a puff of dirt above his head.

Throwing caution to the wind he began running headlong down the steep face of the rise.

Chapter 9

Before Longarm had taken another of his leg-stretching slides down the grade, Blanton's rifle cracked from above his head. The hidden rifleman on the ground below fired again, but Longarm was no longer a stationary target. He'd already begun sliding pell-mell down the embankment. The rifle's lead sang past uncomfortably close to his ear. It thunked into the dirt only an inch or so above his shoulder and so close to his head that the grains of sandy soil raised by the bullet peppered into his cheek and ear.

Another report from Blanton's rifle came hard on the earth-scattering spat of the bullet from below. The ringing of its close passage had not yet died away from Longarm's ears when Blanton's second slug struck the corner of the house, raising a crackling of splintered wood. By this time Longarm had reached a ledge of solid stone, and though it was barely wide enough to accommodate his feet he managed to arrest his plunging course down the steep slope. Now he could shoulder his Winchester.

Longarm saw the rifleman break cover, stepping from behind the big house. The sniper was searching the bluff with his eyes, seeking his target as he swiveled his rifle for another shot. Longarm braced himself as best he could. He knew that he was an easy target and that he had little time before the man below lifted his eyes high enough to spot him.

As Longarm searched hastily for a crevice that he could wedge his boot heel into and begin raising the muzzle of his Winchester, the man on the ground raised his face and saw him clinging. In those few seconds that ticked off while the man below was bringing up the muzzle of his rifle, Longarm's finger squeezed off the round in his own weapon's chamber. His lead flew true. The gunman beside the house took a single involuntary backward step. His rifle sagged in his hands, then dropped to the ground as its owner crumpled beside it and lay motionless.

"Sorry I wasn't covering you the way I ought to've been," Blanton called.

"No need to let that worry you," Longarm replied. "He ain't likely to bother us again."

"And I'd say that fellow was here all by himself," the sheriff went on. "If he wasn't there'd be others coming out of the house by now."

"Likely you're right," Longarm agreed. "This place is too big for just one man, and if anybody else was around they'd have showed up for certain when the shooting started."

"I'll come on down—" Blanton began, then stopped

before going on. "On second thought, maybe I'd better follow along the rim up here until I find a place where I can bring the horses down with me."

"That's a sound idea," Longarm replied. "Stands to reason that there's got to be a horse trail of some kind down to that house, so it'll likely be close by."

Blanton nodded. He was busy gathering the reins of Longarm's mount. Longarm watched his companion mount his own horse and depart, leading the second animal. Even before they were out of sight, he returned his attention to the job of picking the easiest course down the slope.

In spite of his care in making a mental map to follow down the steep slant, Longarm's descent was slow and painstaking. Now and again he could find a surface outcropping in the wide streaks of solid rock that would support one or both of his feet, but these times were rare. More often than not, when his boot heel hit what had seemed a solid ridge, the baked dry footing crumbled under his weight.

On such occasions Longarm was forced to flail and scratch around to find an alternative hold in order to avoid toppling from his precarious position. During much of his scrabbling descent he was fortunate, encountering the crannies and small crevices that he needed, but there were times when he ran into seams of sandy soil that he could span only by stretching his long legs to the utmost and digging his boot heels into the yielding dirt as he took a quick short step downward.

On a few of the frequent stretches of solid stone he found it necessary to lever himself down by hand, one hand locked on the edge of a ledge to hold him in place, the other hand grasping his rifle while he felt for a nubbin of rock or a cleft of some kind in which to nudge his boot toe. Now and then he was forced to move across the face of the cliff on ledges so narrow that he could only inch along by toeing his feet together like a ballet dancer, picking his way across thin crevices between breaks in the stretches of slippery solid stone.

When he neared the bottom of the sheer cliff's face he saw a wide expanse of loose rocks mixed with even looser dirt. The stretch was flat, though it slanted sharply downward toward the house. Longarm began taking giant steps across the crumbly litter. The decline was so steep that he was soon forced to run rather than walk when he reached the final few yards of his descent. Finally his feet were resting on solid level earth. Only then did he look back. There was no sign of Blanton and he assumed that the sheriff was already on the way to join him.

Slipping a cigar from his vest pocket, Longarm flicked a match into flame with his thumbnail, and as he puffed his cheroot to life he began taking stock of the house and barn and the terrain beyond them. He glanced only briefly at the body that lay faceup at the corner of the rambling house. A single quick look told him that the man was indeed dead. There'd be plenty of time to examine him and search his pockets later.

Although the dead man had provided the only sign that the big old ranch house was currently occupied, Longarm moved quietly. He walked slowly and carefully and kept his eyes busy as he began exploring. He circled the house, noting the three trails that branched away from the strip of beaten earth between it and the barn. The hard-baked soil was covered with a thin layer of loose dust, and the faint blurred traces of hoofprints

112

that were visible gave him no certain clue as to the number of riders who'd passed over it. The hoofprints could have been there for hours or days or weeks.

Though Longarm's scrutiny of the desertlike expanse stretching away from the bluff was brief, it was also thorough. Only a few seconds of observation told him that the barren expanse surrounding the house and barn was free from any sign of danger. He started toward the house to give it a quick search, but before he'd reached its door he changed his mind and veered off to head for the barn.

Both of its wide swinging doors were fully opened, but its interior was still dim except for a small patch of light just inside the doors. The spilling brightness illuminated a dirt floor littered with a few stray wisps of hay. Stepping inside, Longarm blinked two or three times to let his eyes adjust to the gloom beyond. As his vision cleared he blinked again, this time unbelievingly. At the far end of the long barn, between the stalls that lined its walls, stood a stagecoach.

"Well, would you just look at that, now," he muttered into the stillness. "It seems like you've found something that a lot of folks in Death and Lordsborough have been wondering about."

Between the narrow slats that formed the partitions separating the stalls he could see the entire space enclosed by the barn, and a quick sweep of his eyes around its interior told him that he was alone in the cavernous structure. He moved quickly, taking long strides across the wide space in the center of the barn until he reached the shafts of the stagecoach. Even in the subdued light that flowed through the wide barn doors behind him he could see that the coach was covered with a heavy film of dust.

"Now, that coach wasn't wheeled in here yesterday, nor the day before, either, old son," he said. His voice had a ghostly timbre as it reverberated in the stillness of the empty barn. "It's been sitting there for quite a spell. Sure as God made little green apples, that's the one that just dropped outa sight a month or so ago someplace between Lordsborough and Death."

Longarm had covered only about half the distance to the coach when Blanton's voice sounded outside.

"Marshal Long!" the sheriff called. "Longarm! You've got to be someplace close by! Give me a hail or show yourself so I'll know where!"

"Come on in the barn, Fred," Longarm called in reply. "I just found something here that's mighty interesting!"

Blanton appeared in the door. Just as Longarm had, he stood inside the barn for a moment, allowing his eyes to become accustomed to the light's change, then started down the wide space between the stalls. He'd almost reached Longarm before he noticed the stagecoach, and as Longarm had before him, he stopped and stared at the unexpected sight.

"You can't have found the stagecoach that everybody's been wondering about this past month!" he exclaimed.

"I'll cover any bet you might feel like making that's just exactly what it is," Longarm said. "And give you double odds to boot. But don't lay your money down, because it's a bet you'd likely lose."

"You've already checked over it?"

Longarm shook his head. "I ain't had time to. I was

114

just starting to look for a lantern when you helloed me."

"All the barns I've ever been in have a lantern hanging up someplace close inside the door," Blanton told him. As he spoke he was turning to look back at the door he'd just entered. He went on, "Sure, there's one on that post by the first stall."

Retracing the few steps he'd taken, the sheriff brought the lantern back. He shook it and the splash of kerosene was faint but unmistakable. Longarm took out a match while Blanton lifted the chimney and turned up the wick. The wide cotton tip ignited at once. Holding the lantern high, they stepped up to the stagecoach.

"I didn't have time to give it any kind of going over," Longarm said. "I just spotted it a minute or so before you came up."

"You can tell it's been here a while," Blanton remarked, running his fingers along the draft pole. As he rubbed his hand over the pole a gleaming streak of varnished wood reflected the lantern light. "It's the one that disappeared from the Lordsborough-Tucson run, all right."

"You can see how come it dropped outa sight, too," Longarm commented, pointing to a pair of bullet holes in the front of the vehicle, close to the driver's high seat. "I'd imagine we'll find a few more like them when we really start looking."

His prediction proved to be correct when they moved to the side of the coach. There were bullet holes on both sides of the stage's body as well as in the door. Reaching inside with the lantern in his hand, Longarm nodded at the dark blotches where dust had collected on the clotted blood that spattered the dusty leather seats.

"There's not likely to be anybody left alive who was

riding in here," Blanton commented. "But I'll bet there's some new graves out on the prairie between here and Lordsborough, even if there isn't much of a chance of finding them."

"Lobo wolves and coyotes have likely been at 'em by now, Fred. Even if we could find 'em, there wouldn't be any way to tell who'd been buried in 'em."

"I suppose you're right. And there wasn't a thing in the coach. I suppose the boot's empty, too?"

"Ain't had time to find out yet, but I'll look now."

Longarm stepped to the back of the stagecoach and lifted the wide leather flap that covered the baggage compartment. Except for two or three spiders busy adding to the webs they'd already woven inside, the baggage space was as empty as the rest of the vehicle.

"It's bare as a billiard ball," he told Blanton as he let the flap drop and stepped up to rejoin the sheriff. "But we got a lot more looking to do before we're finished. Let's go see what that dead man's got on him, and then we'll tackle the house."

Blowing out the lantern, Longarm and Blanton walked to the body of the dead man. He was wearing a black shirt, dark-colored rough jeans and high-heeled calf-high boots. A blotch of blood, almost invisible, stained the shirt. It was already coagulating and darkening in the hot dry air. A thick shock of long black hair spread on the dun-colored earth framed the man's bloodless face.

His unseeing eyes were turned to the sky and his features were frozen in the calmness that comes at the end of life. His face was tanned and smooth, though its dark stubble indicated that two or three days had passed since he'd last used a razor. Between his upcurled lips

116

his front teeth showed a gap where an eyetooth was missing. His nose had been broken at least once, for its bridge was slightly skewed. His filming eyes were dark under brushy brows.

"You recall whether you've ever seen him in your town?" Longarm asked the sheriff after they'd looked at the dead man for a moment.

Blanton shook his head. "I've never arrested him, if that's what you mean. If I had, I'd likely recall him. But I've seen so many just like him on the street or in a saloon that I couldn't tell him from Adam's off ox."

"Well, I sure ain't seen him before that I know of—" Longarm stopped short and a thoughtful frown formed on his face. "But he'd be of a size to match the rider that took those potshots at me when I stumbled onto that wrecked stagecoach while I was riding outa Lordsborough. I never did get a close look at him, not close enough to be sure about him."

"This is the only outlaw hideout I've heard of anywhere close around," Blanton said. "So if you're even halfway sure of this fellow being the same one that shot at you, I'd say there's a good chance you're right."

As Blanton spoke, Longarm was hunkering down beside the dead man. "There just might be something interesting in this fellow's pockets," he told the sheriff. "And we've still got to give the house a good going over."

While Blanton watched, Longarm searched the dead man's pockets, but those of both his shirt and trousers were empty.

"Likely he's got a room in the house where he keeps his truck," Longarm said as he stood up. "We'll likely find his gun belt inside, too. I'd imagine he was indoors when he looked out of a window and saw us coming, grabbed the first gun that came to hand and busted outside. You ready to head inside?"

"I suppose that's our next job," the sheriff put in. "And I don't mind telling you, I'm more than a little bit curious to see just what else we might find."

"It'd be a good idea to stow this fellow away in the barn before we go prowling through the house," Longarm suggested. "And lead our nags in there, too. Ain't no reason to let his friends know they got visitors."

"Sure," Blanton agreed. "No use to spoil a good surprise party."

Picking up the body by the feet and armpits they carried it into the barn and placed it in one of the rear stalls. Then the two led their horses in, put them in stalls, and headed for the house.

Trying the first door they saw and finding it unlocked, they went inside. They'd entered the kitchen, a big room where a cast-iron range hugged one wall, a frying pan and coffeepot on its cooking surface. A cook's wide work shelf filled the wall beside it.

Cabinets stood aligned along another wall and a sizeable table occupied the room's center. Part of the wall was covered by a washstand holding a graniteware basin and an oversized pitcher. A half dozen plain straight chairs were pushed up to the table, though one chair stood askew in front of an unwashed plate that held a knife and fork.

"If you count the chairs, it looks like there's at least six of 'em," Longarm said, indicating the table. "Take away the dead one in the barn, and that likely means five'll be coming back sooner or later."

"Sure does look that way," Blanton agreed. "And no

way of telling where the others have gone or when they'll be back."

"The way it looks now," Longarm went on, "we'll just have to hole up here and wait. But if you look on the good side, we ought to be able to put our waiting to good use. This is a big house, and it's going to take us a while to go through."

"Hadn't we better get started, then? They might be on the way back by now, and may be pretty close to getting here."

"Oh, I ain't overlooking that. And it won't take us long, if we split up. When I was looking down on it from that bluff, I could see real plain how it's laid out."

"I took notice of that when I was riding up. T-shaped," Blanton said.

"Yep. Another room or two off this one we're in, and two, maybe three, butted out from it. Let's go take a look-see and find out for sure."

Blanton was closer to the door than Longarm. He opened it and they stepped into the adjoining room. Their first quick glance told them they'd been right about the layout of the house. The room was twice the size of the kitchen, and an opening near its center led to a hallway.

Though sparsely furnished, containing only a wide bed and two or three easy chairs, it was cluttered with a miscellany of boxes, bundles tied with cord or rope, several valises and carpetbags, suitcases, bulging canvas bags, and other assorted gear. The items were far too numerous and too greatly varied to belong to one person or even a family.

"Loot," Longarm said after his first quick look. "Robbers' loot. And we ain't got time to waste looking at it right now. We'll give it a going over later on, after we've finished finding out about the rooms along that hall."

He led the way into the hall. Three doors stood on each side, all of them closed. Turning to Blanton, he said, "You take one side, I'll handle the other."

Blanton nodded and stepped to the door nearest him while Longarm took the door on the opposite side. A glance told Longarm that his snap judgment had been correct. A tousled bed and a small table with a chair beside it, a tall wardrobe and a chamber pot were the only articles the room contained, except for a pair of battered boots beside the chair and a taggle of miscellaneous clothing on the bed.

Moving on to the second door, he glanced into it, and found that aside from the articles of clothing that were strewn across the bed and floor it was a virtual duplicate of the first. He closed the door, moved to the last room and stepped inside.

This one was different. Unlike the other rooms he'd looked into there was no bed, nor were there any shades or curtains at any of its windows. Instead of a bureau and small table, it contained a large deal table cluttered with small jars of paint, bottles of ink, a scattering of pens and brushes and several stacks of paper. He studied the table's surface for a moment, a thoughtful frown forming on his face. Then his features cleared and he turned back to the door.

Before he could step through it, Blanton came out of the room across the hall. He shook his head when he saw Longarm and said, "I hope you had better luck than I did. All I ran into was three messy beds and a bunch of dirty clothes."

"Maybe I did," Longarm replied. "From what I saw in this room here, I got a pretty good notion we've uncovered a nest of counterfeiters."

"You mean counterfeit money?"

"I sure do." He turned and gestured toward the table as he went on, "All the stuff a good pen artist needs to make fake money's right there on that table."

Longarm was turning back to Blanton when he glanced out the window. In the distance he saw a small group of riders approaching. They were not moving fast, but with the steady gait of men who've traveled many miles. He gestured toward the window.

"Looks like we're about to have company pretty quick. Unless I'm wrong, the gang that uses this place for a hideout is coming home."

Chapter 10

When Longarm made his unexpected announcement, Blanton stepped to the window and joined him in gazing at the distant riders. Although they appeared tiny in the distance, the cloud of dust raised by the hooves of their horses indicated that the men in the saddle were pressing to reach the house.

"Half an hour, wouldn't you say?" he asked Longarm.

"Maybe a little less. They're moving pretty good."

"I suppose you'll arrest them? Or try to?"

"That's what we came here for."

"I count five in the bunch."

"That's what I tallied, too. I grant you, it ain't real good odds, but we've got all the time we need to figure out the best way to handle things. It's lucky the first job we took care of was getting our horses put away in the barn. It ain't likely they'll tumble to us being here, but

123

we got to go out and get our rifles and saddlebags."

"I don't imagine there's one outlaw in that bunch who'd be likely to surrender," Blanton observed as he and Longarm started up the hall.

"Not a chance of that," Longarm agreed. "It'll be a fight, all right, with five of 'em against us. But they won't be looking for anybody to be waiting for 'em here. We've got cover and they haven't. So we got the edge on 'em two ways."

"Well, you're the one to say what we do."

They'd reached their horses by now, and Longarm said, "We ain't got no choice, Fred. I reckon you see that."

"Sure." Blanton's tone was matter-of-fact. "We'll have to take them."

Longarm said nothing while they slipped their rifles from the saddle scabbards and lifted their saddlebags free. As they walked back to the house they were silent until Longarm spoke.

"This ain't like a quick man-on-man shoot-out, Fred. It ain't a case of where a fellow's standing just a little ways in front of a man that draws and he's got to draw himself and shoot fast to keep from getting killed."

"I knew that from the first, Longarm. I've had to face a few of those, when it's draw quick and shoot first, but I never have gone up against a gang that was out to get me, like this bunch will be."

"It ain't quite the same when you got to go by rules that were made by a bunch of lily-livers back East. What the government rule book says is that we got to give them damn outlaws a chance to surrender peaceful."

"And that's what you intend to do?"

124

"Sure. Even if both of us know they ain't about to give in by a damn sight. Unless they shoot first, we got to hold our fire till they get close enough for me to tell 'em they're under arrest and to give up peaceful."

"I guess that means we'll have to let that bunch get close enough to hear you?"

"That's what the rules say. But that don't mean I always go by the rules."

"A man'd be a fool if he did," Blanton said. "Why, those outlaws would be in range before they could hear you."

"Sure. I sorta figured that out myself. But I figured something else out, too. All I got to do is let 'em see me. Now, listen careful and let me lay it out for you."

"Go ahead."

"Soon as they get in rifle range, I figure to let 'em catch sight of me, like I was the fellow that they left behind to look after the place. I'll wave at 'em and they'll likely wave back and keep on coming."

"Suppose they tumble to your trick right away?"

"Why, they'll start shooting, there ain't no doubt about that. But unless I'm real wrong, it'll most likely be a pistol shot, because it takes longer to draw a rifle from a saddle scabbard."

"A pistol bullet kills you just as dead, though."

"That's true as God made little green apples," Longarm agreed. "But it don't make no never-mind. The first move I see any of 'em make for a gun, I'll start moving. Likely that'll be enough to draw their fire, but by then I'll be cutting a shuck back inside while you start shooting. In two shakes of a heifer's tail I'll be back indoors and at my window ready to give you a hand."

"By that time they'll be in point-blank range," Blanton pointed out, "and rifle bullets will go through these wood walls just like they weren't here."

"That occurred to me, too," Longarm replied. "So what we'll do first thing is take the mattresses off of a couple of them beds and prop 'em up under the windows we'll shoot from. Unless one of 'em happens to have a Sharps buffalo gun in his saddle scabbard, which ain't very likely, the wall and the mattress together oughta be plenty to stop a rifle slug."

"We'd better be sure to keep our heads down, too," Blanton added. Then he asked, "One of us at each end of the house?"

Longarm shrugged as he replied, "With just the two of us that's about the best we can do to save our skins. You got any druthers?"

Blanton shook his head. "One end's as good as the other."

"Then you go back to that last room and I'll stay here. You need a hand in wrestling the mattress from the room across the hall?"

"I can handle it by myself."

Longarm nodded and glanced out the window. While he and Blanton had been talking the band of riders had covered perhaps a third of the distance between them and the house. They were more clearly visible, but their faces were still indistinguishable blurs under the broad brims of their hats.

"We still got a little while before they get here, time enough for us to get ready, but not too much to waste. You sure you got it all clear?"

"As clear as it'll ever be. I still think it's a risk, but you're the judge of that."

126

"Then I don't guess there's anything much else to talk about till after the fracas is over."

Blanton nodded and turned to leave the room. Neither man wished the other good luck. To have done so would have broken the unwritten code of the west: that every man is responsible to himself alone, that a job once undertaken must be finished, and that a companion in trouble must be given a helping hand at any cost.

Longarm went to the big double bed and stripped away the tousle of blankets. Tossing them aside he half carried, half dragged the mattress to the window at the end of the big main room. There he upended it and pushed the upper half against the wall beneath the window, bending it as he shoved until it took the shape of the letter L. Its upper half hugged the wall beneath the window and the lower half stretched flat on the floor.

Hunkering down on the bottom half, Longarm gazed out the window to check the progress of the advancing riders. One of the outlaws' horses was limping now and the entire group had slowed down. Although they were much closer to the house, they were not yet close enough to enable him to make out any details of their features.

Sliding a cigar from his vest pocket Longarm lighted it and watched the approaching little cavalcade through a cloud of grey-blue smoke. Slowly the blurred figures of the riders grew clearer until he was able to distinguish the colors of their hats and shirts, but it seemed a long time before he could see their faces in enough detail to think of them as individuals. Even then the wide brims of their hats shaded the riders' faces. He began to think of them in terms of their clothing: blue shirt, black shirt, brown hat, black hat, grey hat.

Longarm waited until the riders were close enough to the point where quick accurate shooting was possible, retreated briskly through the kitchen, stepped out of the house and made his way to the building's corner. As he'd been sure would be the case, the house shielded him from being seen by the approaching riders.

Before peering carefully around the corner of the building Longarm removed his broad-brimmed hat. When he did look, the horsemen were still moving steadily toward the house. They were still too far away to allow him to see enough detail of their features, but his eyes told him that the time had come to spring his trap. He stepped away from the corner of the house and stood where he was sure the oncoming riders would see him at once.

They did see him, almost immediately. The leader waved. Longarm knew that because of the distance they'd mistaken him for the outlaw they'd left behind, and it was not part of his plan to allow them to get too close. He did not return the man's wave. He'd been standing with the butt of his rifle beside his feet, and lifted the weapon now and held it across his chest where it would be more clearly visible and easier to shoulder.

At once the outlaws began tugging their reins to slow down their horses. They began twisting and turning in their saddles. One of them pointed at the house, another began waving his arms. Though the distance was still too great for Longarm to hear even a murmur of their conversation he had no doubt about what had happened. One or more of the outlaws had realized that he was not the gang member who'd been left behind, and he was now the topic of their conversation.

Proof that his assumptions had been right was quick

128

in coming. One of the riders pointed at the house. Long-arm's hand tightened on the forestock of his Winchester. To encourage the outlaws he shifted the weapon back and forth, a gesture he hoped would leave no doubt about the challenge he was presenting.

As he'd been sure it would be, this move had been the one the oncoming outlaws had been awaiting. The outlaw who'd been waving his arms clawed his pistol from its holster and fired without aiming as he brought it up. The slug fell short, kicking up a puff of dust a good fifty yards from Longarm's feet.

It was the shot Longarm had been awaiting. He shouldered his rifle in one swift move and triggered off his shot the instant he got the gang's leader in his sights. He saw the outlaw jerk in his saddle and start to topple.

Dropping the reins and grabbing his saddle horn, the man who'd taken the slug steadied himself as he fought to stay on his horse, but that was his last move. The hand in which he held his revolver was dangling now, and the weapon fell to the ground.

By this time the other outlaws had pulled rifles from their saddle scabbards. The first man to shoulder his rifle let off a shot. The slug whistled past Longarm's head and thunked into the corner of the house.

From the opposite end of the building Fred Blanton's rifle barked. One of the outlaws' horses began limping and trying to buck, and while its rider was clawing for the reins Blanton's follow-up shot took him. Throwing up his arms, he plummeted from his saddle to the ground. The three outlaws remaining were still grabbing for their weapons, but Longarm knew it was well past time for him to take cover. He whirled and dodged around the house and began running for the waiting kitchen door. Above the thunking of his boot heels on the floor he heard Blanton's rifle bark again.

Longarm was in the hall by now and turning to the door of the main room. He crossed the room with two giant strides and dropped to the waiting mattress below the window. Its pane shattered and showered him with shards of broken glass as he was raising his rifle.

Moments before he had put his hat back on, and it had borne the brunt of the showering glass. He removed it again and shook it free of the shards, then flipped it across the room. Longarm had learned long ago that a bare head lifted carefully offers a much smaller target and that a felt hat is not able to stop a bullet.

Curious because no shots had sounded from the guns of either the outlaws or Blanton, Longarm slowly and cautiously raised his head above the windowsill. The remaining outlaws had dismounted now. Their horses were beginning to meander aimlessly around on the barren prairie. Between them and the house he could see the forms of the attacking outlaws. They were stretched flat, keeping their heads as well as their bodies pressed to the ground.

"Waiting time, old son," Longarm muttered. "But it won't do to let up on them bastards out there. And they're likely thinking the same thing about us. It's time to show 'em what's what."

Shouldering his rifle again, Longarm fixed his eyes across the sights. Moving slowly and deliberately, he fanned the muzzle in an arc, seeking a target. He'd passed over the prone and almost invisible forms of the remaining outlaws when out of the corner of an eye he saw that one of the men who'd fallen earlier was beginning to rise to his knees.

With the range already established, Longarm had only to swing the rifle's muzzle back as his forefinger began to close on the trigger. The easy skill and even speed of his movement brought the outlaw into his sights just as the man started to lift his head.

Longarm tightened his finger on the Winchester's trigger. The man's back arched upward when the bullet went home. His head drooped and his rifle fell away from his hands as his body convulsed. The death spasm lasted only a few seconds. The man lurched to one side and lay still.

Before the reverberation of the rifle's muzzle blast had died away, Blanton's rifle barked again. The outlaw who'd raised his head too high when he saw his companion take Longarm's fatal shot was trying to stand up. His movement in levering to his knees ended abruptly as Blanton's slug drilled into him. His torso jerked and for a fraction of a second remained poised. It was his last effort. He dropped flat and did not move again.

Following the flurry of rifle shots silence took over the prairie. The two remaining outlaws were motionless, pressed flat against the ground. Longarm was raising the muzzle of his rifle to send another shot their way when one of the pair broke the silence.

"Don't shoot no more!" he called. "We're ready to give up! You tell us what to do and we'll sure as hell do it!"

Longarm did not reply for a moment, then he called back, "All right! Just don't try no tricks and maybe you'll get outa this alive!"

"That's all we want to do!" the man replied. "You call the turn!"

"Leave your guns laying on the ground and stand up,

131

then!" Longarm commanded. "When you're on your feet, get your hands over your head and keep 'em there!"

Even before Longarm stopped speaking the outlaws were rising to their feet. They straightened up and lifted their arms and stood like schoolboys who knew the harshness of their teacher, waiting to be told what to do next.

"Fred!" Longarm called. "You keep them two covered while I get outside!"

"I've had my sights on 'em all along," Blanton replied. "Go on whenever you've a mind to. They'll move along quiet and peaceful or they won't move at all!"

"Good," Longarm replied. "Soon as I get their guns, you come on out to where we're at. I'll need to borrow the use of your handcuffs."

Longarm leaped to his feet and took leg-stretching strides through the kitchen and along the end of the house. The outlaws were still a dozen paces from him when he stopped. He ordered them to get closer, and when they were within a pace or two distant he raised the palm of his hand to signal that they were to stop.

Longarm did not keep them waiting. He said, "Don't move them arms of yours from where you're holding 'em. Walk slow and easy up here to where I'm standing."

Moving gingerly, the outlaws obeyed. Longarm let them wait while he examined them from their hat tops to their boot soles. Except for an occasional nervous flinching they did not move during his prolonged scrutiny.

"All right," Longarm told them. "One at a time, drop

132

your gun belts." He nodded toward the man nearest him and added, "You first."

Being careful to make no sudden move, the outlaw obeyed. He unbuckled the ornate silver-chased belt and let the weight of the revolver in its holster carry belt and weapon to the ground.

"Now step up to me slow and careful," Longarm commanded.

Moving his feet slowly and gingerly the outlaw stepped forward. As he advanced Longarm took his handcuffs from his belt. When the man was almost within arm's length of him Longarm gestured a command for him to raise his arms. It was obvious that the outlaw had performed the routine before, for he extended his arms, wrists close together. Longarm snapped the cuffs around his extended wrists.

Blanton arrived at that point, carrying his handcuffs in one hand, his revolver in the other. He passed the manacles to Longarm as he stopped beside the already-cuffed prisoner.

"I'll watch him while you take care of the other fellow," he said.

Longarm nodded. Holstering his Colt he started for the second prisoner. The man began unbuckling his gun belt when Longarm began moving toward him. He seemed to be having trouble with the big ornate buckle, and Longarm glanced at his overlapped hands.

He saw the outlaw slide a miniature revolver from its holster behind the buckle. The man was bringing up the tiny weapon and swinging toward him when Longarm drew and fired. The outlaw's body flinched as the heavy slug drove him backward. His fingers tightened and the little revolver spat.

Behind Longarm the other outlaw moaned. Longarm swiveled around to see Blanton turning, too. They watched the handcuffed bandit as he swayed, and saw a trickle of blood seep from the tiny hole just above his brow. He tottered for a moment, then his staring eyes turned upward a fraction of a second before he crumpled slowly to the ground and sprawled in a motionless heap.

Blanton's jaw dropped as he watched the toppling outlaw. Then he turned to Longarm and gasped, "Where the hell did that fellow you were cuffing find a gun that little?"

"There's some jackleg plant back East that's just begun to make 'em. I've only run across three or four. Most folks call 'em whores' guns. The girls like to have 'em handy in case one of their customers gets mean. They ain't but twenty-two caliber, but they'll kill you dead as a forty-five if they hit in the right spot."

"Maybe I wouldn't have believed it if I hadn't seen it, but that accidental shot sure proved it," Blanton commented. He glanced at the bodies on the ground and went on, "I don't suppose there's any doubt about this gang being the stagecoach bandits?"

Longarm shook his head. "Nary a one. But I'd sure like to've had one left alive, to tell us where they got their loot stashed away. It'd be easier if we didn't have to nosey around trying to find it."

"It's in the house somewhere, don't you imagine?"

"More than likely. But let's get these fellows buried proper and eat a bite. Then we'll start looking for it."

134

Chapter 11

After a few minutes of discussion following their fracas with the outlaw gang, Longarm and Blanton had agreed that digging individual graves for the dead bandits would be a needless waste of energy, and now they were finishing the burial of their bodies in a common grave. The dry baked soil had given them trouble at first, but after its surface was broken the digging had been less arduous and they'd soon had the grave prepared.

Longarm tossed a final shovelful of soil on the big square plot of freshly turned earth. He straightened up and drove the spade's blade into the dirt beside him. Leaning on the handle he lighted a fresh cigar as he looked across the broken surface to where Blanton was just swinging his own shovel to strew its load of soil on the hump of prairie.

"Well," Blanton said to Longarm, "this don't look like a grave where half a dozen men are buried. It looks more like a garden somebody's getting ready for spring planting."

"This here's one chore I never did cotton to," Longarm said, raising his voice to reach his companion's ears. "Digging graves and burying dead men."

"I'm not fond of it, myself," Blanton agreed. He moved around the plot of raw soil, stopped beside Longarm and leaned on the handle of his own shovel as he said, "And now there's something else I've just thought about. The horses."

"About the best we can do for 'em is leave the barn door open. They'll hang around the place a while and go back to being wild after a spell. Animals have a way of taking care of themselves."

"I suppose. I get the idea you're ready to call the job finished."

"There ain't another damn thing we can do for them fellows we just put away. Nothing we can do to 'em, either, anymore. They've paid for what they did."

"A pretty good price, too," Blanton added.

"We've finished, so now we got a right to rest," Longarm went on as he took a step toward the house. As Blanton stepped up beside him, he said, "I'll tell you one thing I'm going to do when we get back inside that house."

"What's that?" Blanton asked.

"Sit down in the most comfortable chair I can find and rest a little while. I never was much of a hand with a shovel. Then I figure to eat a bite and go to bed. How does that strike you?"

"In just the right place," the sheriff replied. "I've been thinking along the same lines myself." He nodded toward the declining sun, which was very close to

136

touching the horizon. "If we started back tonight we'd have to stop and bunk down on the desert."

"Oh, we've got a lot of noseying around to do inside before we can leave," Longarm assured him.

"I'd say you're the damnedest man I ever saw to find more work than anybody needs," Blanton said. The smile on his face as he spoke removed any sting his words might have had.

"Nothing but odd jobs now, Fred. Little ones. We need to go through them outlaws' saddlebags and the truck we took outa their pockets. Then there's the rooms they were using and all that forgery stuff we turned up. And we still don't know what all else we're likely to find."

"That can wait until we've had supper, I guess," Blanton replied. "I don't know about you, but I'm so hungry my belly's trying to tell me that my throat's been cut."

"We'll have plenty of time left after we eat to finish up our chores, then we can start out first light in the morning."

"Just give me time to stow away a little grub," Blanton said, "then whenever you say the word we can turn to and get at it."

Longarm ran his hand over the miscellany of objects from the half dozen boxes he and Blanton had emptied onto the table in the back room of the big rambling house. With their stomachs filled and a period of relaxation behind them, they'd decided that in the interest of getting an early start the next day they'd take care of the loose ends that needed their attention that night.

"I don't guess we'll ever know which one of them

outlaws we buried used all this truck," Longarm said to Blanton. "But I sure know what he used it for. This ain't the first counterfeiter's workroom I've run into."

Spread before them on the oversized table were bottles of ink that spanned a rainbow of shades. In addition to the inks they'd unearthed small pots of varicolored paints and pigments, miniature jugs holding alcohol and kerosene, dozens of brushes of different sizes and pens fitted with nibs ranging in diameter from finger-sized to needlepoints. Bags filled with wadded scraps of different varieties of cloth as well as boxes holding paper in a score of shades and textures and sizes stood on the floor waiting further inspection.

In addition to the forger's working tools, Longarm had unearthed a pillowcase stuffed with pieces of the penman's work that had been abandoned while still in various stages of completion. He'd cleared a space on the table and upended the case, then put the bulging pillowslip aside. It had disgorged a shower of paper, mostly small scraps that had been crumpled or wadded up before being stuffed away.

"Might as well rake through this first and get it out from underfoot," he said. "It might be I'll send a wire to Billy Vail, tell him it's here in case the Secret Service decides to send a man down from their Santa Fe office to give it a once-over."

"There wouldn't be much point in that, would there?" Blanton asked. "The man that did the counterfeiting's dead."

"Maybe he is, maybe he ain't," Longarm replied. "We can't be real sure he was put away in one of them graves we dug. He might just be off someplace getting rid of whatever bad money he had on hand."

138

"That hadn't occurred to me. Maybe we'd better take a closer look all over this house before we go. We might turn up some evidence that there are more outlaws in this gang than the ones we buried outside." Rubbing his chin, the sheriff went on, "It's strange that I haven't had any complaints from people who've been fooled about getting bad money."

"You wouldn't be likely to, Fred," Longarm said without interrupting his examination of the papers he'd been going through. "No counterfeiter in his right mind's going to pass bad money close to where he's got his workshop. And if he's like most pen artists, it ain't likely he'd pick a little town like yours. He'd go where enough paper money changes hands that folks would just stuff it in their pockets without taking a close look at it."

"That hadn't occurred to me," Blanton said. "I guess old Baxter Smollet's bank would be about the only place in town where they'd be handling much besides hard money."

"That's right," Longarm agreed. "And—" He stopped short, gazing at a relatively uncrumpled sheet of paper that he'd picked up idly while he was going through the pile on the table.

"And what?" Blanton asked when Longarm did not finish his remark.

"Let's put off talking about fake money for a minute," Longarm replied. He picked up the stack of papers. "I got something here that I'm going to have to think over."

"Something important?"

"It just might be. If this bunch of papers I've got here

is what I got half an idea it is, there was more to that bunch of outlaws than we figured."

"What's in them?" Blanton asked.

"Step over and take a look for yourself."

Blanton moved around the table to join Longarm. He peered over Longarm's shoulder at the sheet he was holding. After studying it for a moment he shook his head.

"I can't even make out what it is," he said.

"It's a sorta scrawled-up mess the way it is now," Longarm agreed. "And likely you don't recognize it because you never had any reason to run into one of these before."

"What is it, then?"

"It looks to me like it started out to be a U.S. Treasury voucher. Except this one ain't real," Longarm went on. "It's a forgery, or what started out to be one. Whoever was trying to copy the real one made some mistakes and threw it away."

"Then where's the real one? The one he was copying?"

"Now, that's a right good question. But if you put two and two together, there's just one answer you can come up with. The real voucher's likely hidden someplace in this house."

"It seems to me like we've pretty well combed the place," Blanton said. "If it really is still in the house, there's not much chance we'd've missed it."

"Let's not be too sure. Remember that them outlaws didn't build this house, some old-timer did. And remember that folks used to keep a lot of money on hand. Banks were few and far between, and there were more outlaws around than there are now, or maybe it just seems that way. Anyhow, a smart rancher generally fixed up a secret place to stow away his cash in."

"That'd make sense, but I'd imagine they did a pretty good job of hiding it, too. You think we'd have a chance of finding it?"

"We'll never find it if we don't try."

"Where do we start?" Blanton asked.

"Far as I'm concerned we've already started."

"Are you saying it might be in this room?"

"That don't quite follow," Longarm replied. He was frowning thoughtfully. "It'd more likely be in that big front room, or maybe the kitchen."

"Well, if we're going to look, let's start back in the kitchen. It's not as big as the other room."

"Suits me. Come along."

Longarm and Blanton walked through the house to the kitchen. They stopped just inside the door and surveyed their surroundings with a careful attention such as they'd never given the room before. When they'd finished their survey Longarm turned to his companion.

"Well?" he asked. "You get any ideas?"

Blanton shook his head. "It still looks like a kitchen to me. How about you?"

"There's just one thing that strikes me," Longarm answered. "Nobody with enough brains to pound sand down a prairie-dog hole is going to put money anywhere a fire might get started, so I'd say it ain't close to the stove. They wouldn't put it in a wall that somebody could get into from outside, so it ain't likely to be along the wall the door's in. It might be between here and the main sitting room. My bet is it's in that little stretch past all them big high cabinets along about where the washstand's sitting."

141

"Then let's move the washstand and find out."

"You just talked me into it. We'll give it a close look."

Followed by Blanton, Longarm stepped over to the wall lined with tall cabinets to the washstand. He peered along the strip between the ceiling and the cabinets, then moved to the small niche in which the washstand stood.

"Let's just pull it out here into the middle of the floor," he said. "It ain't so big that it'll be hard to move."

Longarm lifted the basin and pitcher off the stand and placed them on the stove. Blanton clasped the top corners of the stand and gave it an experimental tug. To his surprise, it rolled toward him so easily that he almost fell backward. When he straightened up and glanced at the section of wall which had been hidden by the stand his eyebrows went up and he turned to Longarm.

"Looks like you're a pretty good guesser," he said with a smile.

Set flush with the wall in the space that had been hidden by the washstand there was a small door with a strip of rawhide tacked to one edge for a handle.

"It wasn't all just guessing," Longarm replied. "And if we ain't found the hidey-hole we're looking for, I'll pull that door off its hinges and eat it without salt and pepper."

Blanton got busy pulling the washstand out of the way of the opening he'd created. He shoved the stand to one side and turned back to Longarm as he said, "Well, aren't you going to open it, now that we've found it?"

"You did all the work. Go on and open the door."

For a moment Blanton fumbled with the leather strip before he got a firm grip on it, then he tugged it and the small door swung open. Both he and Longarm stared. Three narrow shelves spanned the width of the little cabinet behind the door and the bottom of the cabinet made a fourth. A roll of paper occupied most of the top shelf between short neat stacks of gold coins.

All the gold pieces were the same diameter. Longarm took one out and held it close to the lamp. He said, "Double-eagle. All of 'em are, far as I can tell."

Blanton's jaw dropped for a moment. "I never saw this many gold pieces stacked together in my life," he said. Then he added, "Except on the other side of a bank teller's cage. Believe me, Longarm, at twenty dollars apiece, there's one hell of a lot of money in here."

Longarm nodded as he stepped up beside Blanton and inspected the golden hoard. "About fifty to the stack, wouldn't you say?" he asked. He did a quick mental calculation and added, "That'd follow, a thousand dollars to the stack."

"I suppose it would. But I haven't even tried to count them."

"And, let's see," Longarm went on, his eyes busy tallying the number of stacks on each shelf. "The way I make it out, them three shelves including the bottom have each got fifty stacks on 'em, and that top one's got twenty."

While Longarm talked, Blanton had been doing some counting of his own. He said, "My tally comes out the same as yours, then. That's one hundred and seventy stacks of double-eagles. One hundred and seventy thousand dollars, Longarm! And in my book that's more than I'd make if I lived to be two hundred years old."

"Oh, nobody ever said outlawing ain't profitable," Longarm commented. "But that's just too damned much money for a gang in some outa-the-way place like this to steal."

"But the money's there," Blanton pointed out.

"I grant you that. Except it don't smell right, Fred. Why, if that ragtag bunch that's buried out there had pulled off a stage holdup every day of the year, they never could put this much money aside. Not even if all of 'em lived to be a hundred years old."

"Where'd it come from, then? During the three years I've been sheriff I haven't heard of any big bank robberies—safe bustings or holdups either—anywhere close."

"Finding where it came from is what I'll be looking to do as soon as we can get back to town," Longarm answered. "And the quicker we get our chores wound up here, the better I'll like it. But we've been so struck by them stacks of money that we still ain't looked at whatever these papers are up on this top shelf."

While he talked, Longarm was reaching for the roll of papers. He unrolled them and spread them over the flat top of the washstand, then bent forward for a closer look. He studied the one on top for a moment, then lifted his head and turned to Blanton.

"Just like I figured," he said. "Treasury vouchers."

"Paying for silver shipped to the mint?"

Longarm nodded, his eyes on the vouchers. He was separating them, glancing at each one in turn. He reached the last one of the sheaf, looked up at Blanton and said, "This one I'm looking at was to pay for eighteen thousand and something ounces of ninety-nine percent assay silver at eighty-nine cents an ounce. That comes to a little bit more than sixteen thousand dollars."

Blanton whistled before replying, "However you add it up, that's a pretty good sized stack of money."

"I ain't going to argue that," Longarm replied. He was scanning the remaining vouchers as he spoke. When he'd looked at the last one he shook his head and went on, "Well, it ain't quite a million dollars, but when you add all of these together you're looking at damn near that much."

"Just how near is that?"

"So close as to make no never-mind. I don't generally figure up any sums like that, so maybe I didn't tot it right down to the last penny, but it'd be a whole heap closer than farther away from that much."

Blanton's voice showed he was impressed as he said, "And when you add that good-sized chunk that the vouchers cash in for, we've got more than a million dollars right here in front of us."

"Give or take a few thousand," Longarm said. "But even allowing for some bad arithmetic, it's a hell of a chunk of money."

"I don't know what you call a hell of a chunk of money," Blanton said, "but to me that's a small fortune."

"Likely them outlaws figured that way, too, but when you go splitting it up five or six ways it ain't such a much."

"A lot more than either one of us is likely to see."

"Oh, I grant you that," Longarm answered. "But we're alive and them renegades are out there covered with dirt."

"What do we do now?"

"Get a good night's sleep and go on back to town.

145

We won't be leaving at the crack of dawn," Longarm told the sheriff. "I still got a lot of puzzling to do. First of all, I need to look at these vouchers in better light than we have in this room right now. I can't be sure about 'em till after I give 'em a good looking over in bright daylight. After I do that—"

"Hold on," Blanton broke in. "Are you saying those vouchers might be forged?"

"They could be or they couldn't be. If they're forged, the real vouchers will likely be in some hidey-hole we still ain't found yet."

"Let's keep on poking around, then."

"Oh, I aim to do that," Longarm assured him. "Maybe I'm a little bit gun-shy right now, but I aim to do a lot more looking and poking. Between the two, I got half a notion that I'll be getting pretty close to finishing the job I was sent here to take care of."

Chapter 12

"Another half hour oughta see us in town," Longarm said to Fred Blanton. He nodded toward the dark blur of Death on the horizon.

It was the first remark either of them had made for a half hour or more. Both of them had noticed the dark smudge earlier, but neither had commented on it. Bit by bit the indefinite image had begun to take shape, but before it was clearly defined they'd dropped into one of the mottle-floored sinks that broke the generally level land.

As they topped the long upward slant after gentling their horses across the turtle-shelled surface of the sink and reached the flat desert floor again, the town became more plainly visible. By this time they'd put the setting sun at their backs, and even though they were much closer now the town's details were still hidden by the shimmering heat waves that quivered above the barren expanse ahead.

Bit by bit as their tiring horses plodded along patiently they could begin to make out the clutter of houses and stores. And beyond the rooflines of the blurred houses they could also see the bulkier shedlike outlines of the smelter's buildings.

"I won't say I'm sorry to get back," the sheriff replied. "I didn't realize how lucky I am in my job until I got wound up in this case of yours. Are all of them like this one?"

"Oh, some are worse than others. I'd call this case fair to middling. It's a long way from being closed, though."

"We're rid of the outlaw gang," Blanton argued. "And you've got all the Treasury vouchers and coins packed away in your saddlebags. What's left?"

"Loose ends, I guess you'd call 'em. One thing is them Treasury vouchers. I keep on wondering how many more of 'em got forged and cashed in before the ones we turned up. And whose idea it was to work this kinda scheme to start out with."

"You don't think it was the outlaws who started it?"

"That ain't hardly likely," Longarm replied. "I've run across my share of men who were on the wrong side of the law, maybe more than my share. Taking 'em by and large, all they know to do is point a gun at somebody and tell 'em to hand over their money. They don't cotton much to swindling schemes that take a lot of time to bring off."

"Have you got anybody in mind?"

"Right now, I've got everybody in mind," Longarm

148

said with a mirthless grin. "Present company always ex-
cepted."

"I'm glad I'm not on your list."

"You don't qualify, Fred. But everybody in that town
up ahead does. That is, everybody who'd have a chance
to get their hands on one of them vouchers and pass it
on to whichever it was of them fellows we buried that'd
know how to make passable copies of a Treasury
voucher."

"That narrows it down a lot, of course," Blanton
mused. "If I'm right in my guess, you're talking now
about somebody at the bank or the smelter."

"Or somebody who'd handle the vouchers at that
smelter in Lordsborough. They'd know how to do that
kind of job. Or like you said, it might even be somebody in the bank."

"That still leaves a lot of territory to cover."

"Sure. But it goes with the job."

While Longarm and Blanton talked their horses had
been moving steadily ahead. They'd closed the distance
enough now to see the town's buildings as individual
structures instead of vague shimmering shapes. Soon
doorways and window openings took on definition, and
what had earlier been shapeless specks visible only oc-
casionally became riders and pedestrians on the town's
meandering streets.

Longarm broke the silence again. "I've been wondering about them faked vouchers ever since we found
'em, but I reckoned that you'd be doing the same thing
and I didn't want to draw your mind off of what it was
working at. You got any ideas about 'em?"

"I keep coming back to wondering about something."

149

"That something being?"

"Who did the copying," Blanton answered. "If it wasn't one of the outlaws, I guess it might've been somebody in Lordsborough, which is a pretty good sized place, and all the mail coming from the east has to pass through it."

Longarm nodded toward Death and said, "That place is too little for a pen artist to be living in without you knowing about him."

"You're right about that," Blanton agreed. "And I don't know of any. Folks are pretty much alike in this kind of country. Most of 'em have to spend all their time grubbing out a living."

"How about the people that work at the bank?"

"I can see why they'd be the first to come to mind, because whoever did those forgeries had to be copying from the real thing. I know most of the bank people, though, or know about them. There's not all that many, even if the bank is the biggest business in town, next to the smelter, of course. I can't rightly name anybody working there who I'd even suspect of being crooked."

"Well, it looks like I'll just have to do some digging," Longarm said. "Which ain't too unusual in a case like this."

"I'm glad it's your case and not mine. But if I can help—"

"Sure. I'll start poking around again soon as I've had a chance to get rid of the dust and sweat that we're grimed up with, which won't be till tomorrow. Then I'll get busy and keep going till I find whoever it is I'm looking for."

• • •

After he'd left his horse at the livery stable, Longarm draped his saddlebags over one shoulder and headed for the saloon just across the street. Though he had to settle for a milder rye whiskey than his favorite brand, he'd have been willing to accept a shot of bourbon. Almost as enjoyable as the whiskey was the lack of motion and the knowledge that long hours in the saddle had ended for a while.

As was his habit at the end of a journey, Longarm sipped at his second drink while he finished smoking the long thin cigar he'd lighted as a chaser for the first. Feeling reasonably at peace with the world, he picked up his saddlebags and started for the rooming house.

When he'd gotten no response to his discreet knocking on Angela's door, Longarm shaved and luxuriated in a long soaking bath. He'd gotten out of the small cramped tub and was rubbing himself dry when a gentle tap sounded at the bathroom door.

"I'll be out in just a minute," he called.

"Longarm?"

It was Angela's voice. "Nobody else," he answered. "I finally got back."

"I was sure it was you because I've been thinking about you most of the time since I left the house. You're all right, I hope? You're not hurt or anything like that?"

"Not so's you'd notice."

"Are you about through bathing?"

"Pretty near, but I ain't dry yet."

"All the time I was gone I had a feeling that you'd be here when I got back," Angela went on. "Suppose I wait for you in my room?"

151

"Or in mine," he replied. "Then we won't have to worry about one of your renters busting in."

"All of them are gone by now," she replied. "They won't be coming back for a while. We've got the whole house to ourselves, so you won't have to waste time dressing."

"Well, now," Longarm replied, "your room's just a step away and mine's plumb down the hall."

"I'll wait in my room, then."

"That'll suit me just fine," Longarm replied. "I'll be along in a jiffy."

A few more swipes of the towel finished his drying. He could not get Angela out of his thoughts and his groin was already beginning to tingle in the beginning of an erection. In a hurry to dress, Longarm settled for a compromise. Stepping into his long johns, he knotted the arms of the garment around his waist, picked up the rest of his clothing, and took the few steps down the hall to Angela's door. He tapped on it lightly with his fingertips.

"It's not locked," she called. "Just come on in."

Longarm opened the door and slipped inside. The windowshade was drawn, putting the room into a soft twilight dimness. His first quick glance told him that during the few minutes she'd spent waiting for him Angela had taken off her clothes, for she was sitting up in bed with a sheet pulled up around her shoulders.

While Longarm was still blinking to help his eyes adjust to the half-light, she said, "You'd better lock the door, now that you're here. One of the other roomers might not be as polite as you are."

When he turned to face her again after locking the door he blinked again. Angela had moved and was now

152

sitting up watching him. She'd let the sheet fall while his back was turned. Her large firm breasts were fully budded, their dark pink tips pushing out from the dark rosy circle of her pebbled bosom-spots.

"I tapped at your door when I first came in," Longarm told her. "But that was a while ago, and I figured I'd have time to get about twenty pounds of trail dust washed off of me before you got back."

"I stepped out to go to the grocery down the street. I had an idea you'd be hungry and I was out of almost everything."

"I ain't suffering a bit," Longarm assured her. "Not for grub, anyhow."

He was untying the crossed arms of his long johns as he spoke. His burgeoning erection kept them from dropping to the floor, and he was forced to push them down to his thighs before they fell and he could step out of them.

"Then we're both suffering from the same kind of fever," she said coyly. "Each other fever."

"In my book that ain't bad," he replied. "Seeing as we're both here we can cure that mighty quick."

"Let's don't call it anything but catching up," Angela suggested.

"That's as good a name as any," he agreed. "I know I was gone a longer time than I figured to be."

"It seemed like quite a while to me," Angela said. Her eyes were fixed on Longarm's jutting erection. "And from the way you look, you're ready to start making up for the time we've lost."

Longarm stepped to the bed. Angela turned her face up and offered her lips. Longarm met them with his and his mouth opened to her exploring tongue while his hands were caressing the softness of her firm globes, his fingers moving slowly across their dark tips.

For a long moment they held the kiss, clinging together, Angela's hand on the back of Longarm's neck, holding him to her. Her lips were alive, rippling under his. They held their kiss until Angela sighed softly, deep in her throat. Now she let her arms drop to break their embrace and transferred her attentions to his swollen shaft.

Longarm stood looking down at her rhythmically bobbing head, giving her agile tongue and clinging lips free rein for several minutes before he spoke.

"It ain't that I don't enjoy what you're doing," he said at last, "but I won't get no readier than I am now."

As she released him Angela looked up and replied, "Then let's don't wait any longer for what both of us want."

"Maybe we'll enjoy it more because we waited," he suggested. "But whenever you say the word—"

"Now's the word, Longarm! And now's the time!"

Longarm braced his knees on the bed and leaned forward. He fingered her for a moment, finding that she was moistly ready. Angela spread her soft white thighs and Longarm kneeled between them. She grabbed his erection and placed it. He drove into her with a swift hard thrust and held himself pressed firmly against her. Angela squirmed beneath him, heaving her hips up in her effort to take him deeper, gasping in a ripple of small throaty wordless sighs of pleasure.

After he'd enjoyed for a moment the pulsing response that followed his quick full plunging penetration, Longarm began driving. He felt Angela's legs lock loosely around his hips, then she tensed them and began

154

lifting herself to meet his sturdy thrusts. After what Longarm thought was far too short a time Angela began sighing. Her sighs became loud gurgling cries of pleasure, one sigh following the last before its echoes in the room had died away.

Longarm was arching his back now as he stroked and the tempo of his thrusts increased. Angela's arms were wrapped around him, clasping his chest against her firm quivering breasts. She began to rotate her shoulders to enjoy the soft grating of the matted hair against her pebbled rosettes and their jutting tips. All the while her hips were swaying, rotating from side to side as she tightened her locked legs to pull him even more deeply into her when he thrust.

"Oh, this is wonderful, Longarm!" she gasped. "I can't wait for you, but don't stop! Whatever you do, keep right on driving!"

"I'm good for a little while longer," he assured her. "Take your pleasure now. There'll be another time after we've rested a little while."

Longarm felt Angela beginning to shudder as she rose to her climax. He maintained the hard swift tempo of his driving strokes while Angela's body shook and quivered. She writhed and cried out while her hips gyrated even more wildly until her final ecstatic shrieks trailed away and her spastic quivers faded.

Longarm did not stop, but he eased the tempo of his thrusts until he felt Angela begin stirring again. He sought her lips once more and she opened them, responding with her tongue, her panting breaths whistling through her distended nostrils. He saw that she was recovering quickly and as they broke their kiss she gave him quick confirmation.

"You're not through yet, Longarm, and I'm not, either. Just keep going slow and easy until I catch up with you."

"There's not any need for you to try and hurry. I ain't even on my second wind yet."

"Good. The longer you keep going, the better I like it."

Angela bent her knees to widen the span of her thighs and pressed a foot on each side of Longarm's hips. Her changed position spread her crotch wider and allowed Longarm to move more freely. She braced her feet and began to roll her hips from side to side in rhythm with Longarm's lunges. He speeded his tempo and after a few minutes of steady deep driving felt himself stirring.

Angela was responding now with even greater fervor than she'd shown earlier. She grasped Longarm's shoulders and lifted herself bodily to help her bring her hips up faster and even higher than before. Though Longarm did not change the rhythm of his driving he was burying himself deeper with each long downward stroke. Angela opened her eyes and looked up into his.

"You're getting close, Longarm, and so am I. Drive as fast as you want to!"

Longarm was only too ready to oblige her. He speeded up still more, thrusting fiercely to reach his climax. Angela was writhing each time she brought her hips up now and her breathing was growing as ragged as his. His trembling grew to match Angela's and at last he released his control completely to let his own spasm overtake him.

Longarm made a single final thrust and fell forward, his hips still jerking reflexively as he jetted. Angela gasped and a quiver of sound burst from her throat while her wild gyrations peaked and faded, and when the first body-shaking spastic ripples ended she lay quivering feebly under Longarm's inert form.

After their involuntary climactic shudders at last faded away and died, Longarm moved to leave her. Angela wound her arms around him and held him to her.

"No," she whispered. "Stay inside me. Here. We'll turn over."

She rolled onto her side and Longarm moved with her until they lay with one of Angela's thighs under him, the other draped across his hips. Raising her head, she kissed him gently as she said, "It does me good to go to sleep with a man inside me and holding me, but until now it's been a long time since that's happened. You don't mind, do you?"

"Not a bit. I'll likely sleep, too, because we won't be going anyplace tonight except right here in this bed," Longarm said. "Go ahead, Angela. Sleep just as long as you want to."

Longarm awoke drowsily when he felt Angela stirring. He blinked himself fully awake when she began to slip carefully from beneath him and out of the embrace in which they were still intertwined. He made a tentative move to hold her to him but she shook her head.

"You said we don't need to be in a hurry," he reminded her.

"But after your long ride you must be starving!"

"I ain't in any sorta rush," Longarm replied without interrupting his movements. "I sorta like things just the way we are now."

"I'll stay with you, then."

Longarm did not answer. His big hands were closed

157

on her hips, lifting her above him without breaking the fleshly bond that still held them together. Angela had grasped his intention by now. She shifted with him as he turned to lie on his back, and when he settled down she began to rotate her hips slowly.

Now Longarm turned his attention to her breasts. He rubbed his fingertips across the budding tips of her soft full breasts as she continued the measured rotation of her hips. Her moves rapidly increased in tempo, and as they grew faster he locked his hands to keep her twisting in a steady rhythm that preserved their mutual bond.

Angela began gasping. She threw back her head and her body started to quiver in rippling shudders. Longarm began thrusting his hips up to match the peaking of her increasingly spastic moves. He grasped her writhing buttocks to keep their bond intact. Then she began crying out, short sharp moans that soon deepened into a continuing resonance that filled the room.

Her movements grew more fervent, her cries jerkier until they peaked in a final sharp cry. Angela's mounting ecstasy had by now aroused Longarm. He was thrusting upward as best he could and when she began twitching wildly, her cries now a continuing sussurus of sound, he lifted his hips in a last upward thrust and pulled Angela to his chest, locking her in his arms as they trembled through their final moments and then lay quiet.

"Stay in bed if you're still sleepy," Angela told Longarm as she rose from the bed where they'd lain entwined in an exhausted embrace. "I'm going to fix us a bite of breakfast, and I'll call you when it's ready."

"Maybe I can catch up on a few more winks," he

muttered, his eyes only half open. "I'll be along in a few minutes."

"If you don't come out when the food's ready, I'll call you," she promised. She bent to give him a quick farewell kiss and slipped out the door. Longarm closed his eyes and stretched, then suddenly he was asleep again.

He woke with a start and blinked at the sunbathed hue of the drawn windowshade, then rolled out of bed and stepped to the window. All that he could see was the wall of the next house, but that was enough. From the angle of the sun's yellow rays he could see that the day was well along. He dressed quickly and stepped across the hall to the kitchen.

Angela was sitting beside the table. She stood up and went to Longarm, her face upturned for a good-morning kiss. "You were sleeping so soundly when I looked in to call you before that I didn't have the heart to wake you up," she said.

"Well, I'll just get a late start," Longarm replied. "I was figuring on getting to the bank right when it opened up, but I don't guess an hour or so's going to make much never-mind."

"Have you forgotten what day this is?" She smiled. "It's Sunday. The bank's closed."

Chapter 13

For a moment, Longarm stared at Angela in disbelief, then he shook his head and said ruefully, "I sure got my days mislocated. It don't make much never-mind, though. I'll just start at the smelter instead. That Howard fellow's likely there."

"If he is, he'll be by himself," she replied. "The smelter's closed on Sundays, too. Now, sit down and I'll get breakfast for us. You do want breakfast, don't you?"

"Oh, sure. And there ain't nobody I'd enjoy having it with more than you. Now that I'm up, my belly's yelling at me."

"Sit down, then," she said. She moved to the stove and brought back two cups of coffee. "While we're eating you can tell me the things we didn't talk about last night."

"What we didn't talk about was mostly things I

161

didn't find out," Longarm said. "Which is why I was going to nosey around today."

"From the little bit you've said, I get an idea that there's some connection between the town here and those outlaws."

"Now, that's something I ain't sure about yet."

"I still don't know exactly what kind of trouble you and the sheriff got into out on the prairie," she reminded him. "And you've only given me a hint that you found something valuable that might fit into this case you're on."

"Well, to start off with, we ran across that first stage-coach that dropped outa sight a while back. A bunch of outlaws had wheeled it into a barn on the place they were using for a hideout. They came back while we were there, and we swapped a few shots with 'em, but they weren't as gun-smart as they ought to've been. They put up a fight, but it didn't do 'em any good, even if they did have us outgunned."

"You and the sheriff killed all of them?"

"It wasn't such a much of a fracas. I've been in worse ones. Then after we buried 'em we poked around some then came on back here."

"My woman's curiosity must be working overtime," Angela said. "What you said when I first came in about finding something valuable, something that you thought might help you with your case—"

"I just hadn't gotten to that part yet. When we searched that ranch house the outlaws had been using for a hideout, we stumbled over a cache they'd made, at least that's what we figured it was. There was a bunch of money in it, and a bunch of Treasury vouchers that I figure are forgeries."

162

"They weren't the ones you were looking for, then? The vouchers stolen from the stagecoaches?"

"I can't tell which is which," Longarm replied. "But I aim to find out right away."

"And that's all?" Angela asked.

"All that pops into my mind," Longarm said. "But those vouchers have me buffaloed. I have to find out whether they're the real thing or forged ones. If they're just copies made by some crook out to rob the government, then I'll have to run down whoever made 'em before I can close my case."

"I'm afraid I can't help you much in doing that," Angela said, shaking her head. "I've already told you that I don't know of any artists here in town."

"Well, seeing as you've been living here for a pretty good spell, maybe you can do a little asking around. A lot of folks get sorta shy when anybody that wears a badge starts asking 'em questions."

"You know I will, Longarm," Angela assured him. "Even if I don't know exactly where to start."

"Then again," Longarm continued, "if they are counterfeits, that don't explain where the real ones are." He took a sip of coffee and pondered his situation. "This sure is one tangle of a case," he said finally. "Counterfeit or not, I still gotta find out who's behind all this."

"Once you find who's behind it," Angela said, "you'll no doubt find the real ones."

"How do you figure that?" Longarm asked.

"If you'd been the one who stole them, wouldn't you have saved them? Maybe those men knew of someplace where they could eventually sell them, to someone who'd be able to cash them."

Longarm shook his head. "Nobody in his right mind

would try to cash a voucher they knew had been stolen. Them vouchers have all got numbers on 'em, numbers they get from back East. It'd be easy as pie for the Secret Service to backtrail and find out where they came from."

Angela frowned thoughtfully as she said, "The way you put it, those vouchers are just useless pieces of paper."

"That's right," Longarm agreed. "Except—" He fell silent, frowning.

Angela waited until her curiosity got the better of her. Then she asked, "Except what, Longarm?"

"Except to somebody that worked in a bank, somebody that might be able to juggle money around without anybody else knowing what was going on."

"You know that there's only one bank here in town," Angela said. Her voice was as thoughtful as Longarm's. "And old Baxter Smollet keeps a pretty tight hand on everything that's done there, from what I've heard."

"How about that strawboss he's got? That Howard fellow? He seems to have a pretty free hand in running Smollet's mine and smelter. Does he run the bank, too?"

"I can't tell you anything about that," Angela replied. "But you know how I feel about Baxter Smollet. I told you the first time we were talking, when we were having breakfast together right after you got to town."

"Sure," Longarm answered. "And I didn't cotton to him myself when I went to his bank and talked to him, or tried to. Now that I've got something more to go on, I guess it's time for me to have another little talk with Smollet."

"But you said you didn't get anything out of him when you talked to him before," she said.

164

"This time I've got more ammunition. I'll start using it the first thing tomorrow morning, soon as the bank opens up. Now, I tell you what let's do now. Suppose we eat breakfast and go back to bed. Seeing as this is a day off, we might as well make the most of it."

Exhausted by their almost uninterrupted exertions through the course of what had been a very full day, Longarm and Angela were spooned together in her bed and sleeping soundly when the booming reverberation of a shotgun blast shattered the night's stillness.

Longarm was on his feet and reaching for his trousers when a second shot followed. Like the first, it seemed to set the whole house to shaking.

"Those shots sounded like they came from the front end of the hall!" Angela exclaimed.

"They did," Longarm replied. "A shotgun. Sounded like they came from where my room is. You stay right here, Angela. And don't strike a match or light a lamp till I get back. I'm going to take a look-see."

"Be careful!" she called as Longarm went through the door, his Colt ready in his hand.

A night-light on its stand just inside the door to the street filled the narrow hall with a dim glow. Longarm sidled along the wall, his Colt raised and ready. A door opened in the corridor ahead and a tousle-haired sleepy-eyed man stuck out his head.

Before the man in the door could speak, Longarm snapped, "Get back in your room! And stay there till I find out what's going on!"

Other doors were opening now. Longarm raised his voice and called, "Everybody stay put in your rooms! I'll tell you as soon as it's safe for you to come out!"

To the accompaniment of doors slamming and the clicks of keys turning, Longarm sidled ahead along the corridor. He took his room key from his trouser pocket as he moved. Standing at one side of the doorjamb he unlocked the door, turned the knob and flung it open. The room was dark, only the dim glow of the night sky crept in through the window. Outlined against the glow, Longarm saw its curtains and shade fluttering gently in tattered shreds.

Although he was sure of what he'd see in the narrow passageway between the rooming house and its neighboring building, Longarm sidled along the wall to the window, his Colt ready. The dim light trickling in from the low-turned lamp in the hall did not brighten the room enough to silhouette him, but he hugged the wall as he moved carefully to the shattered window.

His bare feet encountered slivers of glass, but none of them cut into his soles. He reached the window. Peering out, he looked along the narrow gap between the rooming house and the neighboring building. As he'd expected, there was no one in sight.

"Longarm?"

At the first sound of Angela's voice from the doorway, Longarm swiveled. In an instinctive reaction he had raised his Colt as he had started his turn. Even before he'd leveled the Colt he recognized Angela's voice and began letting it fall to his side.

"Goodness!" she exclaimed. "I thought for a minute you were going to shoot me!"

"I don't generally let off a shot till I'm sure who it's aimed for," he said. "But I wasn't looking for you. I told you to stay back."

"It's my rooming house," she reminded him. "I was

worried that one of my renters might've been hurt."

"Those shotgun blasts were meant for me," Longarm assured her. After a moment of thoughtful silence he went on, "Both barrels, too. Whoever triggered 'em was real serious about finishing me off. He's long gone by now, though, and I doubt he'll be likely to try again tonight."

By this time their eyes had adjusted to the dim light filtering into the room from the lamp inside the entrance door. Angela gestured at the bed, where tufts of cotton stuck up from the bedclothes in a dozen places.

"He certainly made a mess of that bed," she said. "I hope your gear's all right."

"Whatever's torn up, my travel money will pay for it," Longarm assured her. "But we can figure that out tomorrow. For now, you might tell your renters the shooting's over. I got to get dressed in a hurry and tend to business."

"What kind of business could possibly take you out at this time of night?"

"Even if you and me don't feel like it, the night's still early yet," he said. "I aim to go stir up the sheriff and see if he's got any ideas about who might've tried to put me outa business."

"But, Longarm—" she began.

"Now, don't but me no buts," he broke in. "I ain't going to be gone long, and seeing as how this bed in here's all full of holes and pieces of glass, you and me both know where I'll be looking to spend the rest of the night when I get back."

Angela nodded and turned to go. When she stopped to tap at the door next to his, he squeezed past her and hurried to her room, where he dressed so quickly that he

167

was ready to leave by the time Angela had returned after placating her lodgers.

"I still don't see what you expect to do at this time of night," she argued.

"I don't aim to be gone long, just over to the sheriff's office for a few minutes. Whoever was out to finish me off wasn't from anyplace but this town right here. Now, I figure that since Fred Blanton's been away for a few days, even if it is Sunday he's likely staying in his office late tonight, catching up. There's a chance he might have some idea about who was pulling the trigger of that shotgun."

Longarm found that his hunch had been a shrewd one. As had been the case on the evening of his arrival in Death, lights glowed from the sheriff's office. Even before Longarm reached the door he glimpsed Blanton through the window, bent over a stack of papers on his desk.

"Well, I sure wasn't looking for you tonight," Blanton remarked when he looked up and saw Longarm. "Is this just a friendly visit, or have you run across something in the little time since we got back?"

"Today being Sunday has sorta put a kink in my rope, Fred. But it didn't stop some ornery son of a bitch that tried to fill me full of shotgun pellets a little while ago."

Blanton frowned as he dropped the papers he'd been going through and asked, "Out on the street somewhere?"

Longarm shook his head. "No. He sneaked up in a little sorta alley between my rooming house and the building next to it and poked his gun through the window. He peppered my bed good with his shotgun, only I didn't happen to be in it when he pulled the trigger."

"That means he knew where he was going," Blanton said thoughtfully. "And knew what room you were in. Or thought he did. It was just luck that you weren't."

"I was down the hall a ways," Longarm volunteered quickly, "talking to the landlady. By the time I figured out where the shooting was and got back to my room, he was long gone."

"Since you didn't have a chance to see him, I don't suppose anybody else did?"

"I didn't even bother to ask, but it stands to reason nobody saw him or even knew he was around."

"From what you told me while we were out on the prairie after that bunch of outlaws, you haven't talked to many people here in town," Blanton went on. "Baxter Smollet at his bank, Pat Howard at the smelter, your landlady. Me, of course, and I guess a barkeep in one or two of the saloons. Anybody else you can think about? Somebody you've talked to since we got back?"

Longarm shook his head. "That's about all. I've been going over the same list you just called off, and it sure ain't a long one."

"If there's something you want me to do—"

"There ain't much you can do, Fred. Nor me, either. Not right this minute at least. I was just halfway hoping you might have somebody in mind that I might go looking for tonight. But since that ain't the way of it, about the best thing I can do is go back to my room and get what sleep the night's got left in it."

169

• • •

Following what was at best still only a half-formed plan, Longarm was at the bank's door when it swung open the next morning. He had not been the first to arrive; there were two or three storekeepers and a saloon gambler in a loud checked suit already waiting. Longarm let them enter first, then turned to the clerk who'd unlocked the door.

"I don't reckon Mr. Smollet has come in all this early?" he asked.

"Mr. Smollet sets his own schedule," the man replied. "He has his living quarters on the second floor, and there are times when he's already at his desk before any of us get here. But there are also times when he doesn't put in an appearance for several days."

"And I guess when he doesn't show up, it's Mr. Howard that's in charge?"

"Generally, yes."

"Good enough. It's him I came about anyway. Where is he?"

"He's gone to the mine. This is Monday, and after the hands out there have had Sunday off, there's almost always a few who don't show up. He has to—"

"You don't have to draw me no pictures," Longarm broke in. "I'll just save him and me both some trouble and ride out and talk to him there."

Though it was still early, the morning sun was hot. Longarm was sweating by the time he reached the mine. There were no signs of activity at the mouth of the tunnel that led into the bluff, nor were there any noises coming from the smelter. Dismounting, Longarm walked stiff-legged up the sloping path to the rough arch

170

that formed the mouth of the tunnel and stared into its dimness.

After he'd advanced a few steps the dimness became darker, then the outline of its walls and ceiling brightened. A few more paces and Longarm could see that the brightness came from a lantern set into a niche in the rock-studded earthen wall. As he continued along the rutted hard-beaten floor he soon became accustomed to the lights spaced along the underground passage.

After what seemed a long time he began to hear noises ahead, the dull grating and occasional metallic ringing of tools hitting rocky soil. The sounds grew steadily louder, then the tunnel ahead grew brighter as Longarm entered an immense cavern studded with blobs of light at several points. Dark forms of men swinging picks and wielding shovels told him that he'd reached the face of the shaft at last.

Longarm began moving from one work gang to the next, looking for Pat Howard. In the end it was Howard who found him. The mine boss emerged from a shaft opening ahead just as Longarm was starting toward it.

"Well, Marshal Long, I see you've come back for another look around."

"I ain't just on a look-around visit this time," Longarm replied sternly. "And what I got on my mind don't have too much to do with digging silver outa the ground. It's about some Treasury vouchers that turned up when me and the sheriff cleaned up a nest of outlaws over across the line in New Mexico Territory. Seems you and me have some serious talking to do, Howard."

Howard nodded. "If you've come to ask questions, let's go to the surface where there's less noise. The smelter won't be working until later, so we can go in my office to talk."

"That'll suit me just fine," Longarm replied, thinking to himself that Howard was playing things straight.

Picking up a lantern that stood in the opening of one of the shafts, Howard gestured toward the big tunnel that opened a few paces distant. He motioned for Longarm to join him and they started for the dark yawning tunnel that led to the surface.

As they entered the gloomy shaft Howard remarked, "Since you're not used to being underground, this might help. I'm a bit surprised that you found your way along the stope without a light. Of course, it's not as dark as these old shafts are that lead off of it." Gesturing toward a black blob in the wall ahead, he went on, "Like this one."

Longarm turned to look at the mouth of the tunnel. He heard a brushing noise behind him and started to whirl back, but his move was a few seconds too late. His head jerked forward as the butt of Howard's revolver landed on it, then he knew nothing more.

Chapter 14

Awareness returned slowly to Longarm. He was conscious first that he lay facedown on cold rough ground. Instinctively, he tried to turn over, to find a more comfortable position. The muscles of his arms and legs did not respond as he'd expected them to. His surprise triggered all the instincts and reactions that he'd acquired during his years as a lawman. Memory returned in a flash, and now he not only knew where he was, but who was responsible for his chilly and uncomfortable posture.

"But you can't push all the blame off on that Howard fellow," he muttered as he heaved around to lie on his side. He missed the familiar hard pressure of his holster, and the realization that his Colt had been lifted from it did nothing to boost his spirits. Continuing to speak to the darkness, he went on, "It's your own damn fool fault for being careless when you had more than a little bit of an idea that Howard is a crook."

During the few moments he'd been berating himself, Longarm had continued to strain at his bonds. The thongs Howard had used to bind his wrists behind his back were cutting cruelly into his flesh and each move he made seemed to draw them tighter. His ankles were less uncomfortable since the lashings that encircled them had been wrapped around his boots.

Having found that he could move, though painfully and slowly, Longarm quit fighting his bonds and lay quietly, his mind busy.

"Whatever it is you're hog-tied with is sharp and tough," he said thoughtfully, addressing the darkness. "Rawhide, likely saddle strings. That Howard fellow did a good job, too. Pity you weren't smarter, old son."

During all the time he'd spent analyzing his position and situation, Longarm had been peering blindly into the gloom. His night vision had come to him now and by twisting his neck to the utmost he could dimly make out a few details. The opening of the worked-out stope was a dim formless area of lighter grey than the darkness in the opposite direction. He knew now that his head was pointed toward the depths of the old tunnel.

Flexing his knees, he brought them up and pulled his feet as close as possible to his buttocks. Then he arched his torso until only his head, shoulders, and feet touched the cold ground and, straightening his legs, pushed himself forward headfirst. The maneuver gained him a few inches, and he repeated it. His second effort was more effective, and gained more than had the first.

After he'd repeated the process a half dozen times his head and shoulders were pointed in the direction he wanted to move. At once his task became easier and more effective as well as less painful. By bending his knees and pushing hard with his feet, he could move his head and shoulders a few inches at a time toward the dim patch of grey light. He pushed again and again for a seemingly endless length of time until at last the greyish light took on an amber tinge and he knew that he was near the main tunnel by which he'd entered the mine.

Only a few more minutes of continuous movement were needed to bring Longarm to the main tunnel. He swiveled his head from side to side, hoping that he was close to one of the lanterns he'd recalled noticing when he came in. He saw the glow of one of them at an angle on the opposite side of the broad passageway and inched painfully toward it.

To Longarm the minutes required to push himself on his back to the spot where the lantern glowed seemed like a year. He reached the niche at last and was now ready to attempt the second part of his effort. The shallow wall cavity in which the lantern glowed was far out of reach, its bottom as high as the waist of a man standing erect beside it.

After he'd studied the lantern for a moment, Longarm made his decision. He pushed himself to the niche and rolled to the tunnel's wall, stopping almost directly below the glowing lantern. By much twisting and turning he worked his feet up the wall until his booted toes were within an inch or two of the niche holding the lantern.

Bracing himself as best he could, Longarm twisted around to bring his boot toes to the edge of the shallow depression in which the lantern stood. He placed the toes of his boots at the side of the niche and kicked.

After two tries had failed his third effort succeeded. The lantern wobbled at the next impact of his booted toe, and when he made still another try he succeeded in dislodging it from its shallow resting place.

Longarm started rolling away as soon as he was sure of the direction in which the lantern would fall. It hit the hard earth of the tunnel's floor with a tinkle of breaking glass as its chimney shattered. The wick flared high when the kerosene in the lantern's small reservoir flooded through it. By the light of the flames Longarm saw glass glittering where the shards from the chimney lay on the hard stone-studded ground.

He rolled to the nearest glistening glass sliver and groped for it behind his back until his fingers found it. Then he rolled away from the flames creeping over the floor. Though his fingers had little feeling, Longarm persisted. After what seemed a very long time of sawing on the tough rawhide with the sharp edge of the glass sliver he felt his bonds begin to give. A quick twist of his wrists did the rest. The rawhide strip that bound his wrists parted with a snap and fell away.

"Well, you got outa that fix smelling like a rose, old son," he muttered into the quiet gloom of the tunnel. "Even if you did lose your Colt and—" He stopped short and slid his forefinger into his vest pocket to be sure that his derringer was still in place. Touching the little double-barreled gun reassured him and he went on, "It ain't such a much, but it's saved your bacon before, and it sure is better than no gun at all."

A glance at the flickering flames on the floor told him that they would burn out within a few minutes. He made short work of undoing his leg lashings, then hobbling a bit on limbs that were stiff and only partly manageable, Longarm started toward the tunnel's opening. He wobbled a bit when he walked, and was forced to stop and stretch his legs after he'd taken a few steps.

Although he hadn't counted the lanterns in their niches as he'd entered, Longarm did so now. Beyond the third lantern he saw daylight glowing in the stope's arched mouth. Mobility had been returning steadily to his legs, and his arms had feeling in them again by the time he reached the tunnel's end. His livery horse was still tethered where he'd left it.

Stopping just inside the mouth of the stope Longarm scanned the landscape. Seeing no one, he took a cigar from his pocket and found that his unusual activities had not crushed or broken the thin cylinder of tobacco. He dug out a match and lighted the cigar and stood puffing it while he considered his next move.

Glancing at the sun, Longarm frowned with surprise. Though high in the sky, it was still short of its noon zenith. He began walking down the slope toward his horse, then realized there was no activity at the smelter, no noise coming from its buildings. Longarm frowned, puzzled, until it struck him that there would be no need for the smelter until the miners had been at work long enough to provide the supply of ore needed for it to operate.

Reaching the horse, Longarm mounted and reined it toward the town. Without the familiar weight of his Colt at his hip, he felt just a bit unbalanced as the horse made its steady progress toward the town. He reached Smollet's bank building and reined the horse to the crowded hitch rail, dismounted, and pushed through the door carrying his loot-filled saddlebags.

There were lines stretching back from the tellers'

177

windows now. None of the clerks busy behind the counter that ran the full length of the big room paid any attention to Longarm as he walked slowly toward the door of Baxter Smollet's private office. Through the panes of frosted glass that enclosed the old banker's private domain he could see nothing except the vague form of a man pacing the floor. The whisperlike sounds of voices trickling through the opaque glass enclosure were too muffled for him to make out even a few words of their conversation. Stepping up to the door, Longarm tapped on the glass pane.

Smollet's harsh voice responded. "Come back after a while! I'm too busy to talk to anybody now!"

Instead of replying to the old banker, Longarm turned the doorknob and pushed. The door was locked.

"Damn it, I said come back later!" Now Smollet's voice was raised and angry.

"I'm United States Marshal Long!" Longarm called, his voice raised. "And I'm here on official—" Longarm's sharp eyes caught a shadowed hint of a moving blur through the glass.

Throwing his saddlebags off to the side, he dropped to the floor in the instant of silence that followed his words. He was fumbling his derringer out of his vest as he dropped, but before it was in his hand a gun barked inside the office.

Its bullet shattered the door's glass pane. Longarm got a glimpse of Pat Howard raising his revolver for a second shot. He triggered the derringer. Howard reeled backward, his arm dropping as he moved. The second slug from his pistol struck the tiled floor, and in its ricocheting course it seared a shallow groove in the biceps of Longarm's right arm.

Longarm was rolling away from the gaping door as the bullet reached him. Even while he felt the pain of the heavy slug scoring his flesh, Longarm kept his eyes on Howard while he shifted his derringer from his right hand to his left.

By now the pain of his wounded arm was making itself felt and Longarm lost a moment or two as he made the transfer. He saw Howard swing his revolver and kicked himself into another roll. The lead from Howard's pistol cut a second groove in the floor beneath Longarm's upraised head and splintered the door frame behind him.

Howard was swinging his revolver for a follow-up shot. Longarm got him in the sights of the stubby little derringer and let off his second round. Howard's shoulders twisted around, and Longarm knew that his final shot had not been fatal, for Howard was already turning back as he raised his pistol.

As though it had come from nowhere another shot roared in the little office enclosure. Longarm saw Howard staggering back, his gun hand dropping. Then Howard recovered and dived through the glass partition into the bank's lobby. Looking around, Longarm saw Baxter Smollet lowering a revolver.

"Missed finishing the bastard, damn it!" Smollet growled as he turned to look at Longarm, who was struggling to his feet. "Never was a good shot, anyhow. You in fit shape to go after that son of a bitch? I don't want him to get away!"

"I would be if I had a gun," Longarm replied. He was holding the edge of the office door, using his uninjured muscles to pull himself to his feet.

"Take this one," Smollet said. He extended the pistol

in his hand to Longarm. "It's yours anyway, from what Howard told me. Said he took it off you when he tied you up out at the smelter."

"He wasn't lying about that."

"You got a horse?"

"Sure," Longarm said. "At the hitch rail outside."

"Get after him, then, if you're able!"

"I'm able."

"Then go catch up with him! I want that son of a bitch in jail! From what he just told me, he's been trying to rob me blind!"

"What happened?" Longarm asked.

"The bastard came in here like a crazy man," Smollet said, "waving a gun at me and telling me all sorts of tales. Seems he's been cashing in phony vouchers on my days off. Damn near emptied my safe of double-eagles. That's what I get for trusting anybody but my-self," Smollet added resignedly.

"It sounds pretty much like what I figured," Longarm put in.

"Oh, that ain't the half of it," Smollet continued. "He said he knew you were on to him when you showed up out at the mine. Said all he needed was some money and a head start, and that I was supposed to play dumb when you came looking for him." Smollet slammed his fist down on his desk. "I want that son of a bitch."

"No more than I do," Longarm replied. He was on his feet now. He took the Colt from Smollet's hand. It had a comfortably familiar feel as he restored it to its holster.

"How about that arm of yours? It's bleeding."

"That ain't nothing new to me."

Smollet was pulling an oversized handkerchief from

his pocket. He shook it out and folded it into a triangle, then rolled the triangle into a narrow strip.

"Step over here," he growled. "I'll fix it before you go. You'd play hell riding far, losing blood."

Longarm could see that protesting would be useless. He held his arm outstretched while the old banker pushed up his shirtsleeve and wound the improvised bandage over the bullet crease.

"You've done this kinda job before," Longarm remarked as Smollet tied the ends of the handkerchief together.

"More times than I like to think about. Now, go ahead. Bring me back that two-faced bastard and I'll see he gets what's due him. I don't imagine you're short of shells for that Colt?"

"I got plenty. For my rifle, too," Longarm added. "I'll get back soon as I can. Then we'll straighten out this mess."

Longarm wasted no time pushing his way through the crowd that had gathered around the shattered door and panel that enclosed the banker's office. He ignored the protests of his wound as he hurried to his horse and mounted, then stood up in his stirrups to scan the landscape.

Puffs of dust on the road to the smelter gave him the clue he needed, and where the road rose in a hump halfway to the cluster of buildings he got a glimpse of Howard. The fleeing man was bent over the neck of his mount, galloping hard.

Dropping back into his saddle, Longarm nudged the livery horse ahead. He prodded the animal to a faster gait when he reined it onto the road, and though he caught only a few fleeting glimpses of his quarry he could tell by the occasional rising dust puffs that the fugitive was still ahead.

At the speed which Longarm was galloping the buildings of the smelter quickly took shape. As he drew closer to them Longarm could see the horse Howard had ridden. The animal was standing outside the building which Longarm remembered Howard had described as being unused. He reined in beside the standing horse and stopped long enough to replace the spent shells in his Colt's cylinder. Then he headed for the building.

Reaching the door, Longarm stopped to listen. Only silence greeted his ears for a moment, then he heard the loud sharp thud of something heavy being dropped. Trying the doorknob, Longarm found that it moved freely. He opened it to the smallest slit that would allow him to enter and drew his Colt.

Dropping to the ground, he wriggled snakelike to slide his head and chest through the narrow opening. He stopped with his hips and legs still outside, for the big building had only a half dozen high-set windows, all of them near the top of its walls, and coming in from the bright sunlight made the inside of the cavernous structure seem twilight dim.

For a moment Longarm lay blinking. Though daylight brightened the windows, only a trickle of the light they admitted reached the floor. His eyes adjusted to the dimness and soon he was able to see that rows of huge wooden casks filled the cavernous interior. The casks rose to the height of a tall man's waist and stood in long tiers that stretched from wall to wall with the narrowest of passageways between their rows.

When his eyes had adjusted enough to let him make out the graining of the wooden staves that formed the casks' sides, Longarm snaked his legs inside and hunkered down behind the nearest cask. An occasional scraping noise reached his ears and he risked getting to his feet in order to inspect his surroundings more clearly. His head was still rising above the rim of the cask he'd sheltered behind, and he was turning his eyes from side to side to scan the interior when a shot cracked and a slug splintered the door edge only a couple of inches above his head.

Longarm wasted no time trying to locate the spot where the shot had come from. He pulled himself all the way through the door and stretched out flat, his eyes flicking over the dim interior of the big building as he tried to locate the spot where his unseen enemy had holed up. Nothing moved, no noise sounded.

Raising his voice, Longarm called, "Give up, Howard! There ain't no way you can get away from here!"

His answer was another shot that followed before the echo of Longarm's voice had stopped reverberating through the huge building. This time the slug clanged through the metal wall a foot above Longarm's head.

Longarm did not try to reply with a shot of his own. His mind was occupied with the job of working out a way that would allow him to find his target. It was clear to him now that Howard would not surrender, but his conscience as well as the laws by which he worked forced Longarm to give the fugitive a choice.

"Howard!" Longarm called.

He waited, but no reply came until he'd repeated his shout. Then from some hidey-hole which Longarm had not yet been able to locate, Howard replied, "Go to hell, Marshal! If you want me, you got to find me and face me!"

"You sure that's the way you want it?"

"Damn sure!"

Even before the echoes of Howard's reply died away in the huge building, the fugitive's gun cracked. From the moment the brief echoing of Howard's previous shot had died away, Longarm had been slowly shifting his position into the narrow space between the cask which had been his shelter and the identical cask beside it. The instant the report of Howard's weapon broke the silence, Longarm leaped up, his eyes flicking across the rows of casks.

Though the flicker of motion that he caught sight of lasted for only a second or two, Longarm had succeeded in spotting the location of his adversary, near the center of the last tier of casks. When he glimpsed the flutter of Howard's sleeve vanishing behind a cask on the farthest tier, Longarm held his Colt ready.

Because of the massive casks between him and Howard, Longarm realized he may not be able to get a clear shot at him, and decided to try to coax him into the open. "What happened, Howard," he taunted, "you get tired of taking orders? Get tired of running another man's business, watching him take in all that money every month?"

"That old wrinkled-up bastard never paid me nearly what I was worth," Howard called back.

"So you hooked up with that gang and had 'em steal them vouchers, right? Being Smollet's manager you knew just which stages they'd be coming in on."

Reacting to Longarm's accusations, Howard loosed a wild shot in his direction. Longarm ducked instinctively, but the shot was far wide of him.

"That was your big mistake, Howard," Longarm

continued. "Hell, if you'd been smart, you would've had that gang rob every stage that came this way. Once I realized only the stages with vouchers on 'em got hit, I knew it had to be somebody who knew the schedule. And it only makes sense that a man isn't going to steal from himself, so that cleared Smollet and left you as the main suspect."

Growing more desperate, Howard threw two more rounds in Longarm's direction. Longarm waited patiently, still hoping his prey would make a careless move and show himself.

"And when you clubbed me over the head, that pretty much told me what I needed to know," Longarm went on. "You'd have been smarter just to kill me then."

"I aim to fix that right now," Howard called. Then, like a jack-in-the-box propelled by its spring, Howard's head popped up from the shelter of one of the huge casks on the top-most tier.

Longarm was waiting, his gun hand steady. He had only to correct his aim a tiny fraction of an inch. He triggered off his shot with a steady hand. Howard's trigger finger closed a mere shaving of a second later and he was crumpling, his muscles tensing in their involuntary death spasm. The slug from his revolver thunked into the settling cask that had been his shield as he lurched and toppled to the floor and lay limp in the total stillness of death.

". . . and you can take these damn forged vouchers back with you to Denver, or wherever it is you're going," Baxter Smollet barked, tossing the vouchers on his desk. "I think all the real ones are mixed up in here too.

That should be the lot of them. And remember, if you ever change your mind about coming back here to work for me, don't bother to send me a letter. Just show up and start to work. I guarantee you won't be sorry."

"Well, now, Mr. Smollet," Longarm replied, "I do appreciate your offer, but like I said, I get along pretty good with the job I already got. So now that all my business here's cleared away, I'll be moseying along."

Touching his hat brim in a farewell salute, Longarm walked through the bank and started toward the hitch rack where his horse was waiting. He took longer strides than usual, knowing that Angela was waiting for him.

Watch for

LONGARM AND THE WYOMING BLOODBATH

136th novel in the bold LONGARM series
from Jove

Coming in April!

LONGARM

Explore the exciting Old West with
one of the men who made it wild!